How God Sent A Dog To Save A
FAMILY

How God Sent A Dog To Save A

FAMILY

And Other Devotional Stories

Joel R. Beeke & Diana Kleyn

Illustrated by Jeff Anderson

THE
BUILDING
ON THE
ROCK
SERIES

CF4·K

© Copyright 2003 Reformation Heritage Books
Reprinted 2004, 2005, 2007, 2008 and 2010
Published by Christian Focus Publications
and Reformation Heritage Books
ISBN: 978-1-85792-819-8
Christian Focus Publications Ltd,
Geanies House, Fearn, Tain,
Ross-shire, IV20 1TW.
Scotland, Great Britain
www.christianfocus.com
email: info@christianfocus.com
Reformation Heritage Books
2919 Leonard St, NE, Grand Rapids, MI, 49525
Phone: 616-977-0599
Fax: 616-285-3246
email: orders@heritagebooks.org
Website: www.heritagebooks.org
Illustrations and Cover illustration by Jeff Anderson
Cover design by Alister MacInnes
Printed and bound by Norhaven, Denmark

Building on the Rock · Book Titles and Themes
Book 1: How God Used a Thunderstorm
Living for God and The Value of Scripture
Book 2: How God Stopped the Pirates
Missionary Tales and Remarkable Conversions
Book 3: How God Used a Snowdrift
Honoring God and Dramatic Deliverances
Book 4: How God used a Drought and an Umbrella
Faithful Witnesses and Childhood Faith
Book 5: How God Sent a Dog to Save a Family
God's Care and Childhood Faith

Contents

How to use this book

The stories within this book and the other titles in the *Building on the Rock* series are all stories with a strong gospel and biblical message. They are ideal for more than one purpose.

1. Devotional Stories: These can be used as a child's own personal devotional time or as part of family worship.

Please note that each story has at least one scripture reference. Every story has a scripture reading referred to at the end which can be used as part of the individual's or the family's Bible reading program. Many of the stories have other references to scripture and some have several extra verses which can also be looked up.

Each story has two prayer points at the end of the book. These are written as helps to prayer and are not to be used as prayers themselves. Reading these pointers should help the child or the family to think about issues connected with the story that need prayer in their own life, the life of their church or the world. Out of the two prayer points written for each story, one prayer point is written specifically for those who have saving faith while the other point is written in such a way that both Christians and non-believers will be brought to pray about their sinful nature and perhaps ask God for His salvation or thank Him for His gift of it.

Each story has also a question and discussion section at the end where the message of the story can either be applied to the reader's life or where a direct question is asked regarding the story itself or a related passage of scripture. The answers to the direct questions are given at the end of the book. Scripture references are indexed at the back of the book. Beside each chapter number you will read the scripture references referred to. These include references within the story, question or scripture reading sections.

2. Children's Talks: As well as all the features mentioned above, the following feature has a particular use for all those involved in giving children's talks at Church, Sunday School, Bible Class, etc. At the end of the series in Book 5, you will find a series index of scripture in biblical order where you will be able to research what books in the series have reference to particular Scriptures. The page number where the Scripture appears is also inserted. Again, all Scriptures from stories, question sections, and Scripture readings are referred to in this section

It is also useful to note that each book will have a section where the reader can determine the length of specific stories beforehand. This will sometimes be useful for devotional times but more often will be a useful feature for those developing a children's talk where they are very dependent on the time available.

Shorter Length Stories

The following stories are shorter in length than the average length of story included in this book. They therefore may be used for family devotions, children's talks, etc. where less time is available:

Longer Length Stories

The following stories are longer in length than the average length of story included in this book. They therefore may be used for family devotions, children's talks, etc. where more time is available:

1. A Sermon to One Hearer

Severend Branner once promised to preach for a country minister in England. When the Sabbath came, it was terribly stormy, cold and uncomfortable. It was in the middle of winter and the snow was piled up along the roads, so that travelling was hard. Still, the minister urged his horse through the drifts. He put his animal in the shed, and went into the church. No hearers had arrived as yet. After looking around, the young man took his seat behind the pulpit. Soon the door opened, and one man walked up the aisle, looked about, and took a seat. The time came for the service to begin, but there was only one hearer.

The minister wondered whether he should preach for such a small audience, but he decided he had a duty to do, and he had no right to refuse to do it because only one man would hear it. So he went through the whole service: praying, singing, preaching, giving the benediction, with only *one* hearer. When he had finished, he came down from his pulpit to speak to his hearer, but he had gone away.

Such an unusual event was spoken of

occasionally, but twenty years later it was brought to the minister's mind in the following way:

The minister, being on a journey, stepped down from his coach one day in a pleasant village. A gentleman walked up and said, "Good morning, Reverend Branner."

"I do not remember you," said the minister.

"I suppose not," said the stranger, "but we once spent two hours together in a church alone in a storm."

"I do not recall it, sir," added the older man, "tell me when it was."

"Do you remember preaching twenty years ago in a certain place to only one person?"

"Yes, yes," said the minister, grasping his hand. "I do, indeed; and if you are the man, I have been wishing to see you ever since."

"I am that man, sir, and that sermon was used by God for my salvation. I have become a minister of the gospel, and over there is my church. The converts from that sermon, sir, are many."

Question: Why did Reverend Branner decide to carry on with the service although there was only one hearer?
Scripture reading: Acts 9:1-19.

2. How God Sent a Dog to Save a Family

Mrs Knight sighed. "I'm sorry, but we have nothing to eat. You'll have to go to bed without supper."

"But are you sure, Mom? Don't we have anything?" whined Milly, the youngest child.

"We have nothing, dear. Let me tuck you in. Come on, Emma, Alex, let's go upstairs."

After the children had been tucked in bed, Mrs. Knight sat in the kitchen and read from her Bible. She was a widow who feared the Lord in truth. Providing food for her family was not easy, but she had experienced time and again that the Lord is a "Father of the fatherless and a Judge of the widows" (Psalm 68:5).

Kneeling at her chair, Mrs Knight poured out her troubled heart before her gracious God. She did not complain about the way in which the Lord was leading her. She received grace to submit to God's will. She asked if the Lord would let her children sleep without suffering hunger, and the Lord heard her prayer. They all slept soundly.

But in the morning the children felt their empty stomachs again. It was almost time for school. How could Mrs. Knight send her children to school hungry? She didn't know what to do. "Oh Lord," she sighed, "help us again in Thy mercy. Thou seest and knowest our need."

"Mother, isn't there any bread yet?" asked Alex.

"Not yet, and we have no money either. I don't know how, but the Lord will help us. With the Lord there is deliverance."

The children were silent. Although they were very hungry, they did not complain.

"Come, children," Mrs. Knight said, "let's kneel here and together we will tell the Lord all our needs. We will tell Him that you have to go to school and that we have no food. He knows that, but He wants us to ask Him for these things." Then the mother poured out her heart again in prayer. By faith she was able to plead on the Lord's promise that He would care for His people.

Mrs. Knight was so deeply involved in her prayer that she did not notice what was going on around her. Emma, however, heard a scratching noise at the back door. Finally, she got up and tiptoed out of the room. She opened the door carefully, and gasped in surprise. There stood a dog with a basket in its mouth. In the basket were three loaves of bread! The dog dropped the basket on the mat at the door as though it had strict orders to do just that.

Hearing the commotion, the others came running. What went on in the heart of the widow is impossible to describe. She knew it was the hand of her Lord. True praises to God soon sounded throughout the little house.

The Lord used ravens to send food to the prophet Elijah. In this story He used a dog to bring bread to the praying widow and her three children. Surely the God of Elijah lives! "Happy is he that hath the God of Jacob for his help, whose hope is in the Lord his God" (Psalm 146:5).

Question: How did Mrs. Knight deal with her problem? What other passages of Scripture show you that God has control of animals? What animals are mentioned in Numbers 22:21-35 and Job 39 and 41:1-11? In the Scripture readings look at the different ways God provided food for His people.
Scripture reading: 1 Kings 17:1-6; 2 Kings 4:1-7; 2 Kings 4:42-44.

3. Connie's Chickens

A little girl named Connie lived in the country. Not far from her home, there was a large old barn. In this barn was a hen which belonged to Connie, and when this hen hatched seven little chickens, they belonged to Connie, too.

One evening, just as Connie was going to bed, this barn caught on fire. She saw the bright light flickering through the trees, and soon the whole barn was engulfed in flames.

When Connie's little sister saw this, she began to scream and cry. Connie cried too when she thought of her hen and little chickens. Then she had an idea. She ran to her bedroom, knelt by her bed, and prayed a simple prayer. "Oh God, please don't let my chickens be burned! Please keep them safe! For Jesus' sake. Amen."

The compassionate Savior, who said, "Ask, and it shall be given you," heard that prayer for the little chickens, and answered it. No one ever knew exactly how they got out of the barn, but the next morning, when Connie went out to look at the smoldering ruins of the barn, imagine her delight to see the hen clucking and scratching about, and her seven little chickens with her all safe and sound.

If Jesus heard Connie's prayer, and saved her little chickens from the burning barn, we may be sure that He will hear poor sinners like us when we pray to be saved from that fire which will never be put out.

Question: Have you asked Jesus to deliver you from the punishment of your sins? Scripture reading: Matthew 10:27-31.

4. Doing God's Work

S

In the year 1665, the city of London was struck by The Plague. This was a dreadful disease. No doctors could cure it or do anything to relieve the suffering of the patients. Since it was very contagious, people would leave the city if they could to try to avoid catching this terrible sickness.

Reverend Thomas Vincent lived in London during this time. He did not have a church, but he taught in a school. When he heard that The Plague had reached London, he closed the school, and decided to spend his time visiting the sick, telling as many people as he could about the Lord Jesus Christ. Most of the ministers had left, and Reverend Vincent's friends and family tried to persuade him to leave too. They told him it was too dangerous and that he should not willfully expose himself to such great danger.

But Reverend Vincent refused to go. He believed the Lord wanted him to stay in London. He trusted God, who could protect him from danger if He wanted to do so. Reverend Vincent was willing to die doing the Lord's work, if that was what the Lord wanted.

So he stayed in London. He preached in some of the churches. The people were very happy to listen to him, since so many ministers had left. There were many people who had no relatives living outside of London and who could not afford to pay for an inn. They had no choice but to remain in London, and they were afraid. Crowds of people flocked into the churches.

Death was everywhere. Businesses were closed. Every day, more people became sick, and every day, more people died. Reverend Vincent was very busy visiting the sick, reading the Bible to them, and speaking to them and their families about preparing for eternity.

During that terrible time, nearly 70,000 people died of The Plague in London. Seven people of Reverend Vincent's family died. But the Lord spared Reverend Vincent. He was never sick even one hour during that time. He trusted in his God, and did the work the Lord called him to do. God protected him from danger. "Whoso putteth his trust in the LORD shall be safe" (Proverbs. 29:25b).

Question: How did Reverend Vincent spend his time after the plague broke out?
Scripture reading: Psalm 91.

5. Everything – Even Coal!

Many years ago, people used coal to heat their homes. One winter in Great Britain, there was not enough coal for everyone. The men in the mines were having trouble getting the coal out, so it was very difficult for people to buy it.

During this time, Mrs. Scott, a kind Christian lady, was also faced with the problem of getting coal.

It was Saturday morning. The next day would be Sunday, and the minister would preach a preparatory sermon for the Lord's Supper. She knew that many of God's people came to visit her during the week of preparation to talk about the Lord and His Word. She loved these evenings. But this time she was worried. She needed coal to warm her house.

"I'll go and see the coal dealer in town after breakfast," she said to herself. Then she asked the Lord to help her, telling Him all her needs.

After breakfast, she put on her thick winter coat and stepped out in the cold wintry morning. She hummed as she walked for she was sure the Lord would help her.

But she had a surprise when she came to the coal dealer's shop. Another man was there. He was not friendly, and rudely told her, "Forget it; no coal today. Try again next week."

Mrs. Scott thoughtfully left the shop. She was very disappointed. When she came home, she immediately fell on her knees and prayed to the One who says, "All things are yours." With childlike simplicity and trust she prayed, "O Lord, it is for the comfort of Thy people. Wilt Thou therefore not help? Art Thou not concerned with even the smallest sparrow? Wilt Thou please provide coal for me and Thy children?"

Late that afternoon, Mrs. Scott heard a loud rumbling noise behind her house. Quickly she pulled on her coat and went to see what had happened. To her amazement, she saw that a load of coal had been emptied into her coal bin, but whoever had delivered it had disappeared. Feeling puzzled, she went back into the house, trying to figure out who could have brought the coal. A few moments later, she heard a knock on the door, and there stood two embarrassed coal delivery men.

"We're very sorry, ma'am," said one of them. "We dumped the coal into your box, but we brought it to the wrong address. If you'd like, ma'am, you could pay for it and keep it, otherwise, we can take it back."

Mrs. Scott smiled, "I'll gladly pay for it. You really didn't make a mistake at all.

You've brought it to the right house on the right street! He who reigns in heaven arranged it for me."

The men looked confused and shrugged their shoulders. But Mrs. Scott knew that God had sent the coal to her. She experienced a blessing from the instruction: "Be careful for nothing; but in everything by prayer and supplication with thanksgiving let your requests be made known unto God" (Philippians 4:6).

Question: Why do you think God allowed Mrs. Scott to be turned down the first time? Scripture reading: Matthew 6:26-34.

6. Flying Bread

Wilsie and Waylo sat shivering in their hut. A fierce wind blasted the icy snow down through the smoke hole.

"We may as well admit it," complained Halona, the children's grandmother, "we're going to starve."

The three Indians huddled around the little fire. It burned poorly for the wood was wet. Clouds of smoke stung their eyes.

"I found ten of our sheep dead just now," stated Waylo miserably.

"Ten more?" cried the old woman, "Before this week is over they'll all be dead from cold and hunger. Then there will be nothing left for us to eat." She closed her eyes and began chanting a heathen prayer in her own language.

"Grandma," interrupted Wilsie, "we still have a little bit of flour. I can make two or three loaves of bread. If we eat one slice each per meal, we'll have enough for about four days."

"And then what?" growled Waylo.

"By that time, I think God will have sent help," Wilsie answered cheerfully.

Waylo laughed bitterly. "If I could ride to the white man for help, then maybe God could help us. But now that my pony is dead, I'm stuck here. Grandma's right, Wilsie. If it is the will of the gods that we must die, I am ready."

Grandmother knelt by the fire and fanned the weak flames. It would be hours before the lamb chops would be ready to eat. Waylo tried not to think how good the meat would taste.

Wilsie whisked the snow off an old trunk and took out her Bible. She wanted her grandmother to know the One who could send help from above. Wilsie was sure the Lord would answer her prayer for food. She told the story of Elijah and the ravens. "When Elijah was hungry, God sent ravens with food. Don't you think God will help us if we trust Him?"

"Perhaps, perhaps," said Halona thoughtfully. Wilsie noticed a hopeful look in her eyes.

"I'd like to see that happen," thought Waylo.

The next day was bitterly cold. More sheep died, for they had no shelter from the wind. There they stood, frozen stiff. They had not even toppled over.

"O Lord God, send us help before we die, for Jesus' sake," prayed Wilsie.

"Look!" shouted Waylo, interrupting Wilsie's silent prayers. "Grandma! Wilsie! Come outside! An airplane!"

Sure enough they could hear the faint hum of an airplane.

Wilsie put on her coat and grabbed her red sweater. "Let's wave to them," she shouted. "Maybe they'll see us!"

The children waved and shouted at the tops of their voices, forgetting that the pilots would not be able to hear them. But the pilots had seen them. The men in the little plane were on the lookout for Indians in just such a need.

Halona watched the small yellow plane swoop low over their hut. With tears in her eyes, she saw strong sacks of flour, beans, sugar, and dried fruit being dropped from the plane. Waylo stared open-mouthed as a side of bacon fell a short distance from where he stood. Wilsie jumped aside to dodge packages of coffee and raisins. Indeed, the heavens were raining food!

Halona was not ashamed of her tears as she gathered the food into the hut. There would be enough for the rest of the winter. "It was the white man's God who sent His raven to us," she said, hugging her grandchildren.

Question: God fulfilled the bodily needs of these three Indians. He can do this for you too, boys and girls, but He can also fulfill your spiritual needs. Do you ask Him for this?

Scripture reading: 1 Kings 17:1-16.

7. God is Real

In a hospital room lies a sick man. Sometimes he groans in pain. The nurses do their best to make him comfortable. Presently, the doctor comes to check on him. When he asks the man how he is feeling, the man curses terribly. This makes the doctor very sad. "Don't curse God," says the doctor. "You should pray to God instead of swearing."

"I don't believe there is a God!" answers the man angrily. "I can't see Him, or hear Him, or smell Him, or feel Him."

The doctor is quiet for a few moments. Then he says, "Sir, I don't believe you have any pain. I've checked you out, but I can't find any pain. I can't see it or hear it. You must be lying to me."

"That's not true!" protests the man, "I know my pain is real because I feel it inside!"

"That's how I know God is real," replies the doctor, "because I feel His presence inside me."

Question: How can we know God if we can't see, feel, hear, or smell Him?
Scripture reading: Psalm 115.

8. Jack's Gratitude

L

Many years ago, before cars were invented, people traveled in coaches pulled by horses. One cold night, in a small town in England, a coach stopped at a stable to change horses. Freezing gusts of wind met Henry Williams, the stable owner, as he came out to lead the tired horses into his barn. But as he loosened the harness, a tired, shabby-looking sailor entered his stable. "Excuse me, sir," the sailor said, "but may I sleep in your hayloft tonight?"

"No, never one like you in my barn!" Henry answered roughly. "And you had better keep moving or you will be in big trouble."

"But sir! Maybe you will need help some day, too. And besides, I am honest. I would not take anything that was not mine, even if I were without shoes!"

"Well, I don't trust you any further than I can see you! Now keep moving or else!"

Poor Jack Willis turned away hungry and very tired. He had tried so many places already, but the answer was always the same. No one wanted to help a beggar. As he walked back out into the darkness, someone touched him lightly on the shoulder. Turning, Jack saw a young boy who had been helping in the stable. "Wait!" said the boy quietly, "I think I know where you can get help. Just go down this road to the first little shop you come to. Mrs. Smith is a widow, but I'm sure she will let you sleep in her woodshed. She is very kind and is always willing to help those who need it."

"Thank you very much!" replied Jack. What a feeling of warmth filled his heart! There was still someone who cared enough to help the needy.

Jack's ship had come into port only two days before. But when he reached shore, Jack was robbed of all he had. Now he had to beg his way to London. And every time someone refused to give him food or shelter, it hurt him deeply.

Jack moved quickly down the street. His heart was filled with hope, but when he reached the shop, the door was locked. It was quite late already. Did he dare to disturb Mrs. Smith? Jack hesitated, but he remembered what the stable boy had told him about how kind she was. She never sent people away without helping them. Jack softly knocked on the door. His knock was soon answered with, "Good evening! Were you looking for me?"

"Hello. Are you Mrs. Smith? I was told that if I would ask you, that you might let me sleep in your woodshed."

"Why, come in! You look as though you are nearly frozen. I don't have much to share tonight, but won't you join me? I was just sitting down to eat."

As Jack shared the widow's simple meal, he told her about everything that had happened. He told her about some of the shipwrecks he had seen. He also related how he had narrowly escaped becoming shipwrecked himself. "Well, Mr. Willis, how thankful you must be that God in His providence has spared you until this very moment! But remember that He who has saved your life at sea can also save your soul. The Lord has sent His Son, Jesus Christ, to die for the sins of His people. Have you asked the Lord to have mercy on you?"

After giving thanks to the Lord for the meal, the widow spread some clean, dry straw in a corner of her woodshed. With a thankful heart, Jack lay down upon the straw and slept soundly all night. When he woke up the next morning, he straightened his rumpled clothing the best he could. Then he went to thank the kind woman who had cared for him. But instead, he found that she had prepared a warm breakfast for him. When the meal was finished, she also gave him a small sum of money to help him travel farther. As Jack left her home, Mrs. Smith wished him the Lord's blessing on his way.

Ten years went by, and no one remembered what had happened on that cold, windy night. No one, that is, except one person. Many changes had taken place in that small town. Mrs. Smith, too, had grown older. Her hair was whiter and she needed a cane to walk. But she still had a heart filled with love for helping others. Even though she was not rich, she still shared what she had with those who needed it.

One morning Mrs. Smith received a large, very important-looking letter. "Dear Mrs. Smith," it read, "You are invited to come to London tomorrow. I have a message for you. But I want to give you this message in person. Please meet me at 11 a.m. at the Red Lion Inn. Thank you."

Mrs. Smith was very puzzled by this invitation. "Don't go, Mrs. Smith," said her neighbor. "Someone is just trying to play a trick on you."

"I don't think it would be proper for you to go to such a meeting by yourself. You know, London is a very wicked place!" said another neighbor. "I'm afraid that someone will harm you in some way."

Mrs. Smith had never been away from her own little town. She was a bit afraid to go on such a long journey. But she was willing to believe the best in everyone. The Lord had opened her eyes to see her need for His Son, Jesus Christ, for her salvation. And she also trusted that God in His providence would protect her from all harm.

So the following morning, Mrs. Smith took the first coach to London. The driver helped her from the coach, and soon she stood inside the great Red Lion Inn. But before she could become worried, two respectable-looking men greeted her. "Well, Mrs. Smith," said the one, "I'm very glad to see that you were able to make the trip. Please come with us to our room." When reaching their room, Mrs. Smith was very surprised to hear the same man say, "Well Mother, how are you doing? Don't you remember me?"

Mrs. Smith looked carefully at the stranger. "No, sir. I don't believe I do," she hesitated.

"I am Jack Willis. Remember the begging sailor you took into your home about ten years ago? I had no money and no friends in a strange town. But you gave me food and a place to sleep that cold, wintry night. I have never forgotten your kindness. And now that I am the captain of a larger ship, I wish to give you something in return." Turning to the other man, Jack continued, "This is Mr. Bates. He is a lawyer whom I have asked to pay you a sum of money each year at this time. This is to show something of my thankfulness to you for your kindness. But, especially, I want you to know that your warning words were used by God to speak to my heart. The Lord used your words and examples to convict me of my sin. He has also led me to the only source of salvation for such a sinner as I am—to His Son, the Lord Jesus Christ."

Mrs. Smith's heart was filled with wonder.

Overwhelmed by all that she had heard, she burst into tears. Giving thanks to God for His rich blessings and care for Jack in both body and soul, she returned to her own home. How thankful she was that the Lord had provided also for her! She now had enough money to help even more needy ones. But for the rest of her days, whenever she listened to someone tell of their troubles, she always thought of God's wonderful providence and grace as witnessed in the life of Jack Willis.

Question: What part of Mrs. Smith's help was Jack most grateful for?
Scripture reading: Luke 17:11-19.

9. God Lives

Once there was a minister's wife who trusted in God. In times of trouble she often said, "Do not fear; God lives, and He will take care of us."

But after her husband's death, life became very difficult. They were so poor, and often the children were sick. But she still believed that God lived and would care for them.

One day, however, when things were particularly difficult, her faith failed and she burst into tears. Her youngest son saw her crying. He put his little hands into hers and looked into her tear-stained face. Very sadly he asked, "Mommy, is God dead now?"

Startled, his mother stopped crying and dried her tears. She took her little boy into her arms and said, "No, my son, God is not dead. Thank you for asking that question. He always lives. He is an ever-present help in every time of need. He will help us."

God used her little boy to remind her that He lives and remains faithful to His people.

Question: Why was it a comfort to the minister's wife that God lives?
Scripture reading: Isaiah 41:1-13.

10. Johan Brentz

Johan Brentz was almost eighteen years old when Martin Luther nailed his ninety-five theses on the church door in Wittenburg in 1517. He lived in a city in Germany named Halle. He was a God-fearing man, and his influence in the church and state of Wurttemberg was great. The Roman Catholics, of course, did not like this at all. They hated him.

In the year 1546, the inhabitants of Halle received fearful news. Emperor Charles V had sent the Duke of Alva with an army to capture the city and persecute the Protestants. The Duke of Alva had his mind set on one particular person—Johan Brentz. When Halle was taken, the Duke gave his soldiers the command to find Brentz and bring this "heretic" to him, dead or alive. The cruel soldiers rushed to the home of the preacher. Brentz was startled when he heard them pounding on the front door, but he quickly made up his mind to leave. Just as he ran out the back door, he heard a soldier's axe come crashing through the front door. But Brentz was safe. The soldiers searched the house, but could not find him. When the Duke of Alva left with his soldiers,

Brentz returned to Halle and preached again the gospel of Jesus Christ.

When Charles V heard this, he was furious, and was determined to capture Brentz, whatever the cost.

June 14 was Brentz's birthday, and he was enjoying a birthday dinner with his family. Little did he know that he was in great danger.

Granvelle, an officer sent by Charles V, rode into Halle with his army, with the purpose of arresting Brentz. Granvelle went straight to the city hall. As soon as all the council members were seated, he told them that the emperor had a secret message for them. Naturally they were eager to know what this message was.

"First you must swear solemnly that you will not tell anyone what I am going to tell you," said Granvelle.

The men swore an oath of secrecy. With a sly smile, Granvelle took the emperor's letter out of his pocket and read it aloud. Johan Brentz was to be taken prisoner. If the gentlemen would help him capture this "heretic," the emperor would reward them, but if they did not help him, the entire city would suffer.

With a fright the councilmen realized they had been tricked. The cunning Granvelle knew that Brentz had many friends among them, and for this reason he had sworn them to secrecy. This way, they would not be able to warn the pastor of the danger.

The councilmen felt trapped. They did not want to betray their beloved minister, but at the same time, they were afraid of the emperor's revenge. Fear gained the victory, and they decided to help Granvelle.

Granvelle was sure now that Brentz would not be able to escape. Quickly he sent a soldier to bring Brentz to him.

But Granvelle did not consider that God's fatherly eye watched over Brentz. When the gentlemen swore an oath of secrecy, Granvelle had not noticed that one of the councilmen was missing, but had entered some time later. As soon as this man learned of the plan to arrest Brentz, he wrote a short note.

Brentz was still sitting at his birthday dinner when the messenger brought this note. He opened it and read, "Flee! Flee! Flee!"

Quickly Brentz changed his clothes and left the house. In the street the preacher met the soldier who was on his way to arrest him. He stopped Brentz and asked him, "Do you know where Johan Brentz lives?"

Calmly Brentz answered, "Yes, I do. Let me show you." He walked back a short way with the soldier and pointed out the parsonage at the end of the street. Then each continued on his way, the soldier to the parsonage, and Brentz through the town gate to another city called Stuttgart.

The duke who lived there, Duke Ulrich, welcomed Brentz with open arms and hid him in his palace. But it was not long before a traitor told Charles V where Brentz was hiding. Immediately the emperor sent a Spanish troop of soldiers on horseback to bring Brentz to him. The soldiers began their journey, stopping one night at the elector of Bavaria who served them a delicious meal and offered them beds to sleep on. At the meal, the officer in charge explained the purpose of their journey. "We have orders from Charles V to bring the heretic Johan Brentz to him, dead or alive. We found out that he's hiding at the palace of Duke Ulrich in Stuttgart. We plan to surprise him. He has no idea we're coming."

The next day, the horsemen rode into Stuttgart. The officer went at once to Duke Ulrich and demanded, "Bring out Johan Brentz immediately! I know he's hiding in your palace. These are the orders of Emperor Charles V." It was plain that the officer was sure of success. But if he thought he would surprise the Duke, he was mistaken. It was the Duke who surprised him when he answered, "He is not here."

"Well, where is he then? I know he's here!"

"I honestly do not know where he is," replied the Duke.

When the officer eyed him suspiciously, he added, "It's the truth, sir. I have no idea where he is. I can swear to that."

Angrily the officer rode away, wondering how Brentz could possibly have discovered their intentions.

But God who rules over everything also took care of His child in this attempt to capture him. The previous night, when the soldiers were having dinner at the home of the elector of Bavaria, the officer had proudly told him his errand. The elector's wife had heard it too. The officer did not realize that this lady was a friend of the preacher. Since the officer had clearly stated that Brentz was hiding at the palace in Stuttgart, she sent a message to Duke Ulrich.

It was late at night when the Duke received the message. Quietly he woke Brentz. "You must flee once more, I fear. A traitor has informed the emperor where you are hiding. Tomorrow his soldiers are coming to arrest you. You must leave immediately. Don't tell me where you are going, for then I won't be able to tell the soldiers anything. May God travel with you and greatly bless you, Brentz."

Brentz embraced the Duke and left the palace, taking only a loaf of bread with him. Brentz was thankful for the warm night and soft moonlight. An owl hooted nearby and a little animal scurried for safety somewhere in the dense undergrowth. Brentz passed unnoticed through the heavy palace gates and then stopped. Where must he go? Suddenly overwhelmed with sorrow and confusion, he fell on his knees and begged for the Lord's assistance. Then he took the road that led him through seemingly endless beechwoods. Here and there stood a little house, but all the doors were locked, except for the last one. It was as if he heard a voice whispering, "Go into it."

Guided by the moonlight, he crept softly up the stairs into the attic, without the occupants of the house noticing. Brentz thanked God as he settled on the floor of the attic. He drifted off to sleep just as the first streaks of dawn crept over the horizon.

When he awoke several hours later, he looked around to see where he was. A few feet away from him lay a great heap of twigs. Brentz decided it might be better if he went over to the other side of this pile. Without a sound he made his way over the sticks and then noticed a heavy beam in the far corner of the attic. "What an excellent hiding place," he thought. He sat down behind the beam, ate some of his bread, and then listened for any sounds that could tell him where he was and what was happening.

Some time later, he heard the unmistakable sound of hoofbeats. His heart beat a little faster. It must be the emperor's troop who were coming to capture him! The people in the neighborhood stood outside talking about it, and Brentz could understand every word. Then the voices faded away and the people wandered farther down the road.

A few hours after this, the preacher overhead the people talking below him. "Is it true that the gates of the city will be closed?" It was a woman's voice.

A man's voice answered, "Yes, that's true. The soldiers are going to search every house in this village. They are determined to catch the heretic!"

Late in the afternoon Brentz heard some rustling in the pile of sticks. He laid down beside the beam and held his breath. The sound came nearer and nearer until it was right beside him. Slowly, Brentz turned his head to see what it was. Then he smiled at his fear. It was just a chicken! But soon he was filled with fear again when the chicken laid an egg. "Now the chicken will cackle and someone will come to find the egg, and so discover me."

The chicken, however, did not cackle, and the preacher's fear changed to thankfulness at the goodness of the Lord. The chicken tripped away as quietly as she came. Brentz was reminded of the prophet Elijah, to whom the ravens brought bread and meat at the command of God. He ate the egg with a piece of bread, firmly believing that the Lord would care for him.

And God did care for him. Every day the chicken returned and laid an egg without cackling.

But the Spanish troop was coming closer. Brentz heard the people talking downstairs. "Today the soldiers will search our neighborhood." Sure enough, the soldiers soon appeared at the house, not even stopping to knock before they entered. The preacher entrusted himself into the care of his faithful Savior and forced himself as far into his hiding place as possible.

Presently, soldiers went to the attic to see if perhaps the heretic was hiding there. They looked everywhere. One of the men poked his sword several times into the pile of sticks, and another jabbed at the thatched roof.

"He's not here," grumbled one.

"March on!" was the command, and the troop left the house.

It had been fifteen days now that Brentz had been in his hiding place. Each day the chicken had laid an egg near him. On the sixteenth day, the chicken did not come. The troops also left the city the same day. Brentz heard this from the people downstairs. He waited until dark, and then quietly left this remarkable hiding place.

Brentz made his way back to Duke Ulrich's palace. How surprised the Duke was to see his dear friend once again! How great was his admiration at the wonderful way in which the Lord had chosen to protect and feed Johan Brentz.

Not human strength or mighty hosts,
Not charging steeds or warlike boasts
Can save from overthrow;
But God will save from death and shame
All those who fear and trust His Name,
And they no want shall know.

Question: Which Bible character did the chicken's eggs remind Johan of?
Scripture reading: 1 Samuel 23:13-29.

11. God's Care for a Little Boy

S

Many years ago, the yellow fever swept through New Orleans. This was a terrible sickness from which many people died. A man on his way to work noticed a little boy lying on the grass beside the road. The man stopped and asked, "What are you doing?"

"Waiting for God to come and take care of me," replied the boy.

The man was touched by the sadness in the boy's voice. He also noticed that the child did not look well. "What do you mean?" questioned the man.

"God sent for my mother and father, and my little brother too," explained the boy. "He took them away to His home in the sky. Mommy told me before she went that God would take care of me. I have no home, and no one to take care of me, so I came out here to look in the sky for God. He will come and take care of me, won't He? Mommy told me He would."

The man's eyes filled with tears. "Yes, my child, God will take care of you. He has sent me to take care of you. You may come home with me."

A beautiful smile lit up the child's face. "I

knew that God would take care of me!" he cried. "Mommy was right!"

God rewarded this little boy's trust in Him. The man took this boy into his home and loved him as one of his own children. The Lord never disappoints anyone who trusts in Him.

Question: Do you love and trust the Lord Jesus Christ?
Scripture reading: Proverbs 3:1-12.

12. Martha's Raven

Martha Randall lived alone in a small house in the country. It had been five years since her dear husband, John, had passed away. Now she was no longer able to work and had become very poor. Martha's life had been very hard; she felt very alone in the world. Her only living relative was her nephew, Bruce. He lived only a mile away with his wife, Betty, and their three children. Bruce had a good job and was very rich, but did not bring any comfort into his aunt's life.

Martha was an elderly, God-fearing woman. She had learned to trust the Lord for all things. Even though she was lonely and poor, she was content. But Bruce, with all his wealth and comfort, did not know the meaning of true happiness. He hated religion and mocked his aunt for her simple faith in God. He could not understand how she could find so much happiness in the Lord.

As winter approached, Martha's supplies became very low. Then the weather turned very cold, and a heavy snowfall made it impossible for her to go out. Each day she allowed herself to eat only as much as necessary. But the time came when she had to eat the last of her food. Her last half of a potato, together with a bit of milk, was all she had for breakfast. Then her cupboard was empty. But she did not complain. The Lord had always supplied for her needs in the past and she was sure that He would help her again.

That evening, Martha began to feel very hungry. "It would be so wonderful to have a piece of bread before going to bed!" she thought. She did not see how it would be possible on such a stormy night. But she had just finished reading a chapter in the Bible. One text was very comforting to her: "All things, whatsoever ye shall ask in prayer, believing, ye shall receive" (Matthew 21:22). Martha knelt beside her bed and prayed for bread. She read these beautiful words again and then repeated her prayer.

That same evening, Bruce stopped for some extra groceries on his way home from work. Several friends were coming for dinner the following day. Betty had made a list of items she needed, including six loaves of bread. The way home led past his aunt's home. "I think I'll just stop by to see if the old lady is still alive!" he thought. He got out of the car and walked quietly up to the door. Opening the door just a bit, he peeked into the room just as Aunt Martha closed her eyes to pray for the third time. Bruce stood silently outside her door and listened. "Dear Lord," she prayed, "my food is gone and I am hungry. Thou hast said in Thy Word that whatsoever we shall ask in prayer, believing, we shall receive. Please give me some bread." Bruce had heard enough. Quietly he returned to the car, chuckling to himself. Here was a great opportunity to play a joke on his aunt! He had always told his friends, "When I want something, I have to work for it. But Aunt Martha says she can get things by praying for them!" Now he had heard such a prayer. Now he would show her how wrong she was!

Taking a loaf of bread from the car, Bruce went back to the house. He quietly slipped inside and placed the loaf on the table. As he drove away, he could picture how Aunt Martha would tell people tomorrow how God had sent her a loaf of bread. Then he could prove to her that he had given her the bread. He could tell her how silly it was to pray to God!

Martha ended her prayer and opened her eyes. There on the table was a loaf of bread! With quiet joy she gave thanks to Him who was faithful to His promise.

The next day as dinner time approached Martha received another surprise. Someone in her nephew's car drove up her lane. As she watched, a boy got out and came to the door. He handed her an urgent message. "Aunt Martha," the note said, "we want you to join us for dinner. Come immediately." Martha did not know what to think, but quickly changed into her best dress. With some fear she went with the boy to Bruce's car. The short drive to her nephew's house, however, filled her heart with joy. The beautiful snow lay sparkling on the trees, fences, and rooftops. She no longer troubled herself to wonder why her hateful nephew had called for her.

When she entered the house, she was immediately taken to the dining room. Bruce and his family and several friends were already seated at the table. "Well, well, Aunt Martha," her nephew said in a mocking tone. "I thought we should have you come to dinner today so you wouldn't starve!" A hot meal was placed before her, and she bowed her head to ask a blessing on the wonderful meal. Martha could feel that Bruce and his friends were ridiculing her, but she ate her meal, giving thanks in her heart to God.

After the meal was finished, Bruce spoke to his aunt again. "So today at least you have had a good meal. But what about yesterday?"

Martha looked up and answered sweetly, "I have never been forsaken. The Lord Himself provides for His children."

"That's what you always say," Bruce snorted. "But how does He provide? Just give me one example if you can!"

"Why certainly," Martha replied. "Just last night I was fed as miraculously as Elijah was fed by the ravens!" Bruce had told his friends about the trick he had pulled on his aunt. So now Bruce and his friends began to laugh.

"Tell us about it," Bruce said, glancing around at his friends with a smirk.

Aunt Martha looked up bravely and told everything that had happened. "Last night I had nothing left in the house to eat. I was very hungry, so I asked the Lord to send me some bread. I prayed for a long time, but at last I arose from my knees. I'm sure you will only laugh, but there on the table was a loaf of bread. I divided that loaf into three parts, so it would last me for three days. I thanked God with every bite I took from my first portion."

Now Bruce burst out with laughter. "But I am the one you should thank; I placed that loaf of bread on your table myself." All his friends joined Bruce in laughing at his aunt.

After the laughter had died down, Martha looked at her nephew and calmly said, "Elijah did not thank the ravens, Bruce."

Sudden silence filled the room. Bruce flushed in anger and muttered, "You're just an old hypocrite. Just go home, and I hope I never see you again!"

With quiet dignity Martha replied, "I would not have come if you hadn't invited me, Bruce. I thank you for what you have given me. For the rest you must answer to God." So saying, she quietly left the room. As she reached for her coat, however, Betty joined her. "Let me help you with your coat," Betty offered. Soon several guests respectfully gathered around her, too. How sorry they were to have made fun of this godly woman! Seeing how things had turned out, Bruce ordered the car to be brought. Martha was driven home in comfort.

The Lord richly blessed Martha's testimony of faith. The next morning Betty came to Martha's home and said, "I was very impressed with what I heard you say at the table yesterday. Won't you please pray for me? I am such a sinful person; I miss what you have. Please teach me how to pray."

Martha's heart was filled with humble gratitude to God. She prayed that the Lord would guide her in explaining to Betty the way of salvation which the Holy Spirit works in the hearts of needy sinners.

Question: Why did Martha give thanks to God for what Bruce had given her? Many Christians find Nehemiah 8:10 a help in times of trouble. What emotion is mentioned in this verse?
Scripture reading: Esther 8.

13. "Our Father in Heaven"

There was once a family who lived on the Isle of Wight in England. The family consisted of Mr. and Mrs. Winslow, and one little girl named Lily. Mr. Winslow had gone to America to buy a farm and build a house before he returned to escort his wife and daughter to their new home in a new country. He had written that everything was ready and that he hoped to be home for Christmas. Then the three of them would sail for America.

But Christmas came and went without Mr. Winslow's return. Day after day and week after week passed, but still he did not come home. Mrs. Winslow and Lily, of course, were very worried. At last, the sad news reached them that the ship he had sailed on had been wrecked, and that all on board, except for three sailors, were drowned. What a dreadful blow that was to Mrs. Winslow and little Lily!

At the end of the first day after hearing the news, Lily kneeled down by her mother's side to pray before going to sleep. Mrs. Winslow was crying, and tears streamed down Lily's cheeks as well. She tried, between sobs, to say the words she had been taught. Almost before she knew it, she found herself saying, "God bless my dear father."

Mrs. Winslow stroked her daughter's head, and said, "O Lily, my darling, you can't say that anymore. You have no father anymore."

Lily was silent. She didn't know what to say. Then she began to recite the familiar words of the Lord's Prayer. "Our Father, which art in heaven." How beautiful those words seemed to Lily then! She felt she had never truly understood their meaning, or how sacred they were until that evening. She stopped a while to think about them. Then she said them over again. She said them a third time, "Our Father, which art in heaven." Then she looked up into her mother's sorrowful face, and said, "Oh, Mother! We do have a Father! God is our Father! Jesus said so. He told us to pray to 'our Father in heaven.'" Then she said these precious words once more.

Lily couldn't say any more of the prayer. These words were enough. The grieving mother and daughter found comfort in the knowledge that they had a Father in heaven who couldn't be drowned, who never sleeps. He is the best Father.

Questions: Do you love this heavenly Father? Do you know Him?
Scripture reading: Jeremiah 31:1-14.

14. "Send Food To John"

On top of Washington Mountain, overlooking a deep valley, stood a simple hut. This hut was the home of John Barry, a poor charcoal burner. During the past summer, John had felt sick and was not able to work as much as usual.

In December, several heavy snowfalls came. The road up the mountain from the village below was completely drifted shut. Before the road could be cleared, another storm raged, and John and his wife were stranded with only one day's supply of food left.

In the village of Sheffield, ten miles away, lived Deacon Brown. Mr. Brown was a well-to-do farmer, known for his Christian life and practice. The deacon and his wife, Margaret, had gone to bed, and, in spite of the storm, both were sleeping soundly. Toward morning, the deacon suddenly awoke. He had a strong impression he needed to bring food to someone named John. He awoke his wife and told her.

"Nonsense!" replied Mrs. Brown. "Go back to sleep. You must have been dreaming."

The deacon laid down again, and in a

few minutes he was asleep. When he awoke, the impression was as strong as ever.

"Well!" said Mrs. Brown, "You must be ill. I wonder if you have a fever. Lie down and try to sleep."

"Listen, Margaret," he said, "Do you know anyone named John who might need food?"

"No one that I can think of," replied Mrs. Brown, "unless it could be John Barry, the old charcoal burner on the mountain."

"That's it!" exclaimed the deacon. "Now I remember. When I was at the store in town the other day, Mr. Clark said, 'I wonder if old John Barry is alive, for it is six weeks since I saw him. He has not come in for his winter stock of groceries yet.' It must be that old John is sick and needs food."

Quickly, the deacon and his wife got dressed. Mr. Brown woke his helper, Willie, and the men ate a hurried breakfast while Mrs. Brown packed a good supply of food in the two largest baskets she could find.

After breakfast, Mr. Brown and Willie hitched up the horses to the double sleigh. With a month's supply of food, they began their journey just as the first streaks of light apeared on the horizon. It would be a dangerous trip. The wind was still blowing and the snow kept falling and drifting. Yet the team of horses continued on their trip of mercy, while the people on the sleigh, wrapped up in blankets and extra buffalo robes, urged the horses through the drifts in the face of the storm. That ten-mile ride, which normally took less than an hour, was not completed until nearly five hours had passed.

At last they drew up in front of the hut where the poor, trusting Christian man and his wife had been praying for help to Him who is the hearer of prayer. As the deacon reached the door, he heard the voice of prayer. He knocked at the door; it was opened, and we can scarcely imagine the joy of the old couple! The generous supply of food was carried in, and thanksgivings were raised to God by John Barry and his wife in their mountain hut.

Question: Can you think of a Bible character who received food in a remarkable way?
Scripture reading: Acts 9:10-19.

15. The Chimney Sweep

About two hundred and fifty years ago, boys often worked as chimney sweeps. They had to climb inside chimneys to scrape and sweep away the soot. This was hard and unhealthy work for these unhappy children.

This is a true story about a little chimney sweep named Charles. Charles's parents were the Earl and Countess of Belville. That meant that the King of England had made Charles's father a ruler over a county called Belville. The Earl of Belville died when Charles was very young, so the Countess was left to raise this child alone. She loved him very much. Her greatest desire for Charles was that he would receive a new heart from the Lord while he was still young.

But it seemed that the more she prayed for Charles's conversion, and the more she talked to her son about the Lord Jesus, the less interest he showed. He was disobedient and stubborn, and always tried to change the subject when his mother taught him from the Bible. He daydreamed whenever the Word of God was read to him, and paid no attention when his mother prayed aloud at mealtimes.

This made the Countess very sad and she often cried, but she did not punish Charles when he was naughty and rude. This only made him more daring in his sinful ways.

One day, the Countess was sitting in her little study, writing a few letters, when a servant entered. He waited impatiently until she looked up.

"Madam," he said nervously, "we can't find Charles. We think he is lost. We've looked for him for more than an hour."

The Countess's face turned pale. "What? Oh, not my little Charles! Did you tell the police? Did you really look everywhere?"

Servants were sent throughout the city to try to find the little boy, and the police were notified. The Countess even had some papers printed describing her son and offering a large reward to anyone who could help find him.

Several people came to tell the Countess that they had seen a boy that matched the description, but when the police investigated, he always turned out to be another child.

Finally, a woman came and told the Countess she had seen a little boy about five years old throwing stones into the river. When she had returned a short time later, the boy was gone.

The Countess was heartbroken. She knew Charles loved to go for walks to the river. She had always forbidden him to go there alone, for she was afraid he would fall in and drown. She tried to tell herself that that was what happened, but somehow she could not believe that her dear son was dead.

Three years passed by without any news of Charles. "He would be eight today," she thought sadly on his birthday.

The Countess looked carefully at each little boy she met, sometimes stopping them eagerly. She was always disappointed.

That summer she went to visit some friends in the country for several weeks. She had arranged for some repairs to be done to her home and she would rather be away while this was taking place. But after three weeks, her friends received a message that their daughter was very sick, and that she wanted them to be with her. They offered the use of their home while they were gone, but she decided to return to Belville.

When she arrived at her home that afternoon, the servants and some painters were hard at work in the dining room. Then she noticed a little boy leaning against the wall near the fireplace. He was very thin and pale, and large tears left white streaks on his dirty face.

"What's the matter, little boy?" asked the Countess.

"Nothing, ma'am," answered the boy. "We are cleaning your chimney. My master is on the roof checking to see that I did my job okay. He'll be down soon."

"But why are you crying?" persisted the Countess.

"Because... because...." The little boy tried to talk, but soon was shaking with sobs.

"Tell me what's wrong, child," soothed the lady.

"I'm scared my master will beat me again," he said tearfully.

"Does he beat you often?"

"Almost every day, ma'am."

"But what for?"

"Because I don't make enough money." He kept looking toward the door, afraid his master would hear him. "When I come in at night after I've been out all day, and nobody has asked me to clean their chimney, then he says that I've been playing all day. But that's not true. It's not my fault if nobody asks me! I call as loud as I can, and I knock at people's doors, but nobody wants me to clean their chimney."

"But sometimes you do get work, don't you? Does he beat you then?"

"Yes. He says I don't climb fast enough, or that I don't make them clean enough, or that I made a mess in the house. When I come down he hits me, but I always do my best. Yesterday I hurt my leg, and my breaches ripped." The poor child cried as he showed the Countess his badly scraped leg. The Countess asked a servant to get a bandage for him.

"How much do you earn?" continued the Countess.

"Nothing, except he gives me my food, but it isn't enough. I go to bed still hungry."

"I think I will talk to your master about this," she said.

"Oh no, please don't, ma'am!" begged the little chimney sweep. "He will just beat me again when we are gone. I don't complain to anybody, only at night to...."

"To whom?" asked the Countess eagerly.

"To God."

"What do you say to Him?" The Countess gently cleaned and bandaged the sore leg as she spoke.

"I ask Him to take me back to my mom," he answered, the tears filling his eyes again.

"So you have a mother," the Countess said softly, as though to herself.

"Yes, I do. She is a very nice mother. I wish I could go to her. Then I wouldn't be so sad."

"Don't you know where she lives?" the Countess seemed surprised.

"No. All I can remember is a big house and a nice yard with a wall around it." He stopped and looked around him. "It was like this house — I could see lots of trees out of the windows. My mom was like you, except she didn't wear black clothes."

Lady Belville suddenly felt weak all over, and sat down in the nearest chair. Taking the boy by the hand, she drew him to her side, not minding at all his grimy clothes. Then she asked, "Has the Lord ever answered you, my child?"

"Not that prayer, but I am sure He will hear me one day."

"Why are you so sure?"

"Because He has said so in His Word."

"So you believe that God hears prayer?"

"Yes, ma'am. He has already heard some of my prayers. I prayed that I could learn to read, and that I could have a Bible. A nice man gave me a New Testament one day, and he taught me how to read a little. Sometimes I feel so happy when I pray."

"You feel happy? What do you say in your prayers then?"

"I say the prayer that my mommy taught me by heart."

"And what was that prayer? Say it for me." Lady Belville's heart was pounding.

The little boy knelt at her side, folded his hands and closed his eyes from which a few tears escaped. In a trembling voice he said, "Lord, convert me, and change my heart. Teach me to love Thee and to love others as Jesus has said. Amen."

"My child!" cried the Countess, hugging him close. "You are my son!"

Charles looked at her with an expression of bewilderment on his tear-stained face.

"I am your mother," she said, sobbing aloud. Then she knelt down beside her son and exclaimed from the fulness of her heart, "Oh Lord, forgive me for having offended Thee by my unbelief, and for doubting Thy promise. I have been so impatient. I have prayed so often for his conversion, but I was so unwilling to wait, and yet Thou hast heard me."

At this moment Charles's master entered the room, and was very much amazed at seeing the little chimney sweep and the lady both on their knees. The Countess asked him to explain how he had gotten Charles in his possession.

The man told her. "A man came to me one day and said he was the boy's father. He'd give him to me if I paid him a hundred dollars. The last I heard of him was that he was very sick. Perhaps he's dead now, I don't know."

When Lady Belville explained that Charles was her son, the master seemed suddenly in a hurry to leave, realizing he could be imprisoned or fined for such an offense. The Countess got the address of the man who had sold Charles, and that same evening, she went to see him.

The man was rude, and cursed loudly when she asked him to tell her how he had found Charles. At first he pretended to know nothing about it, but when the Countess kept questioning him, he admitted that he had kidnapped Charles, who had jumped over the garden wall. He then sold him to the man Charles was working for. The man was afraid the Countess would inform the police, but she was so happy to have her son back that she told him she forgave him. She left a tract for him to read, and returned home with a song in her heart.

Every year since then, the Countess celebrated this happy day in an unusual way. The servants found as many chimney sweeps as they could, washed them, gave them new clothes, and brought them into the dining room. There they were served a delicious meal. Afterwards, Lady Belville told the remarkable story of her lost son. She told these children how the Lord had answered her prayers and Charles's prayers in such a wonderful way.

The Countess tried her best to find better jobs for the older boys, and good homes for the younger ones. Many times these boys would come to thank her for her kindness to them, and sometimes they could also tell her what the Lord had done in their hearts.

Question: How did the Countess know for certain that the chimney sweep was her son?
Scripture reading: Luke 7:11-16.

16. The German Carpenter

Hans Graaffe had grown up in Germany. His father was a skilled and respected carpenter, and had taught his sons the trade. But when Hans wanted to marry a young woman from a very poor family, Mr. Graaffe became angry.

"If you marry that girl, Hans, never come here again! You will not get one penny from me, and I won't work with you anymore!"

Deeply hurt by his father's harsh response, Hans and his new bride left Germany and settled in Plymouth, England. He rented a small place and set up shop. But it was hard to find work, as work was scarce. Things became worse and one day, Hans wondered if praying might help. So he prayed. He asked God to help him and give him work so he could buy food for his growing family. Soon he did get work and Hans was pleased. He decided to ask again.

During the next few weeks, however, his prayers seemed to go unanswered. Instead, he began to see that he was a sinner, and had no right to God's help. He began to pray for mercy.

When Hans was a boy, he went to church and learned that Jesus Christ forgives sin. When Hans' mother died however, his father stopped attending church, so Hans had only a little knowledge of the Bible.

"How can God forgive me?" wondered Hans. "If only I had a Bible! I wonder if the Bible has stories about people as sinful as I am, and if they were forgiven."

Then he thought, "God has answered my prayers for food so many times. I am certain He will hear me if I ask Him for a German Bible that I can read."

For many months Hans prayed every day for a German Bible, but no Bible came. Then one evening, as he prepared some wood at the door of his house, two men passed by. They were speaking in German. Hans called to them and discovered that they were two brothers on their way to London, but they had neither food nor money. Hans told them he was poor too, but that they were welcome to stay for supper and spend the night with him and his family. Gratefully, the travelers accepted Hans's generous offer.

The next morning, the men spoke of leaving, but Hans persuaded them to stay for lunch. "I will sell some of the products I make; then I can buy food and you will set out after a good meal."

"I wish," said the older of the two brothers, "that I had something to give you for your kindness, but I am poor."

"It is no shame to be poor," answered Hans. "The Lord Jesus Christ Himself was poor. I wish you knew how to pray to God. He would provide for your needs."

"My mother taught us some little prayers, but I have given up saying them," said the younger brother with a laugh.

"Oh, that is not what I mean," responded Hans. "My prayers are put into my heart by God. Like you, I often repeated prayers from memory without thinking, but only that which comes from God can go to God."

"Well, if God has not given me prayer, I cannot have it, according to you; so it is no fault of mine," reasoned the young man.

"It is often our sin which causes prayers to go unanswered," explained Hans quietly. "That is why it is so sweet to get what I need from God when I ask Him for it."

"You don't get much!" retorted the older brother.

"My poverty does not trouble me. My sins do," said Hans sadly. "I wish I could know my sins are forgiven!"

"Why don't you pray for it then?" asked the younger man with a mocking smile.

"I do," answered Hans, "but God will not be hurried."

"Well," said the older brother, "I do not understand you, but we thank you for your kindness. If we could repay you, we would. We have nothing of value, except an old German Bible."

Hans was stunned. The older brother untied his bundle and took out the Bible. Hans took it in his hands and pressed it to his chest, tears of joy and thanksgiving rolling down his cheeks. "He does hear my prayer! Oh, what a God is my God!"

The travelers stood amazed at Hans's emotion, and were even more surprised to hear that Hans had been praying for a German Bible for eight months.

"It would have been kind of God to give it to me without prayer," remarked Hans, "but it was far kinder of Him to teach me to pray for it."

The brothers went on their way, deeply impressed by God's obvious answer to the German carpenter's prayers.

Hans studied God's Word and found forgiveness with Him, and joy in His service. Eagerly, he taught his wife and children the precious truths of the Bible.

Dear children, "With God all things are possible" (Matthew 19:26). Not only that, but "He is faithful that promised" (Hebrews 10:23). God has promised you that if you ask Him to forgive your sins and to help you love Him with all your heart, He will do it for Jesus' sake. And God always keeps His promises.

Question: Do you treasure your Bible the way that Hans did? Do you pray to God? Read Nehemiah 2 to find out about Nehemiah's prayer. What does it tell you about prayer?
Scripture reading: James 1:1-12.

17. The Stolen Sleigh

It was the winter of 1829 when a man named John Cotton* moved into the small town of Marshfield, Vermont. He found a place to live, and tried to earn his living by selling clocks as well as working for a farmer. When he had lived in Marshfield for about six weeks, he asked his neighbor, Mr. Preston, if he could borrow his horse and sleigh for three days. Since people in these small farming communities were always willing and ready to help one another, Mr. Preston cheerfully agreed.

But, after four days, the Preston family began to worry. There was no sign of John Cotton. Had he gotten into an accident? Or could he have stolen the horse and sleigh? Mr. Preston decided to find some information on John Cotton. Since there was no sheriff for miles around, Mr. Preston questioned some of the people John Cotton had talked to or sold clocks to, and discovered that the man owed several people quite a bit of money. Mr. Preston also learned that the man had stolen several things from the farmer he had worked for.

"He's been gone four days, Preston," said

* Not the famous Rev. John Cotton of New England

75

Mr. Bennett, the farmer. "There's no way you could catch up to him, let alone track him."

Sadly, Mr. Preston nodded his head in agreement. Losing a horse and a sleigh was a severe blow to a struggling pioneer family.

"I'd be glad to loan you a horse," offered the farmer, "but I don't have an extra sleigh."

"Thanks, Bennett," responded Mr. Preston, accepting the offer gratefully. "I'll pay you as soon as I can."

Mr. Bennett only smiled and nodded, knowing how difficult it was to pay for even the smallest necessities. But he gladly gave Mr. Preston the horse.

"God will care for you and your family," said the farmer.

"Yes, He will," agreed Mr. Preston, but he was worried. How was he to pay Mr. Bennett for the horse? And how was he to buy a sleigh?

Three weeks passed, and still there was no word from John Cotton. One evening, coming in from doing the chores, Mr. Preston smiled at his wife.

"I will not worry about my sleigh and my horse anymore. I believe the Lord will return them to me again," he said calmly.

"Why do you think that?" asked his wife.

"I have been praying about it," he answered. "I've asked God to stop John Cotton, so that He will arrange for me to get my horse and sleigh back somehow. I believe the Lord will answer my prayer."

Mr. Preston was filled with the peace that the Lord only can give His people. He had cast his burden on the Lord, and now trusted the Lord to right a wrong.

Several days later, Mr. Preston took Mr. Bennett's horse and rode into town to get some supplies. He made a stop at the post office while he was there. Among his mail was a letter with a postmark from Littleton, New Hampshire. Puzzled, Mr. Preston opened it. His heart filled with thankfulness when he read the short note:

"Mr. Preston, I am the innkeeper here in Littleton. Since John Cotton cannot write, he's asked me to tell you that he has left your horse and sleigh here. Come to the inn here, and ask for John Niles."

Quickly Mr. Preston returned home to share the happy news with his wife. Together they made preparations for Mr. Preston to make the trip to Littleton. The following day, Mr. Preston left for the forty mile trip to Littleton, where he found his horse and sleigh safe and sound. John Niles, the innkeeper, told Mr. Preston what he knew of the strange story.

"Last week, at around midnight, John Cotton came here asking for some supper. He wouldn't stay till morning, but wanted to leave again as soon as he could. But he wanted to leave the horse and the sleigh here and asked me to write you that note. He seemed very uncomfortable, and explained that he had wanted to use the horse and the sleigh to pay off a debt he owed someone. He left at about two o'clock in the morning, riding an old horse he had tied to the back of the sleigh."

John Cotton never paid the debts he owed any of the other people in the area, and since that time, no one ever heard anything about him again.

See how the Lord provides for His people! See how the Lord teaches His people to put their trust in Him, even when things seem humanly impossible! "Be careful for nothing; but in every thing by prayer and supplication with thanksgiving let your requests be made known unto God. And the peace of God, which passeth all understanding, shall keep your hearts and minds through Christ Jesus" (Philippians 4:6-7).

Question: What was the key to Mr. Preston's peace of mind and the eventual return of the sleigh?
Scripture reading: 1 Samuel 5:1-6:16.

18. After Many Days

Little Ronnie Walters quickly finished dressing. It was Sunday morning and Mother was already waiting for him. They lived in the city of Glasgow, only four blocks from church. It was a beautiful day, so they would walk to church this morning.

But not everyone was planning to attend church that morning. As Ronnie walked along holding his mother's hand, two very rough-looking young men came staggering past them. Dressed in dirty clothes, and seeing Ronnie neatly dressed for church, the men laughed loudly, and began to sing a song full of profanity.

Ronnie pressed closer to his mother, wishing the men would disappear. But to his surprise, Mother said, "Ronnie, quickly run after those men and invite them to come to church with us." Ronnie could not believe his ears. Why would Mother say such a thing? But willing to obey, Ronnie fearfully ran after the two men calling, "Wait! I want to talk to you!"

"Well, what is this? The little gentleman wants to talk to the likes of us. What do you want, kid?"

Timidly, Ronnie answered, "Mother says

you are invited to attend church with us this morning. You can sit in our pew."

"Attend church? Hah! Never in your life!" said one of the men as he turned away. Then swearing terribly, he staggered on his way down the street.

But the other man hesitated. He started to follow his friend, but then turned back to Ronnie. Looking thoughtfully at the little boy he said, "You know, Sonny, when I was about your age I went to church every Sunday. Now I haven't been to church for many years. But I don't feel right about it. I believe I will go with you."

Now Ronnie was no longer afraid. He was happy that the man had agreed. Taking his rough hand, he led him back to Mother.

Together they walked into church and sat in their usual place.

Rev. Coates was preaching that morning. The young man listened as the minister read his text. "Our text for this morning's service can be found in Ecclesiastes 11:1 where we read, 'Cast thy bread upon the waters: for thou shalt find it after many days.'" Rev. Coates then preached a very powerful sermon about man's duty towards God and his neighbor.

As he listened, the stranger seemed to become very discouraged and unhappy. After the service, Mother asked him, "Sir, do you have a Bible?"

"No," he answered, "but I will try to get one."

"Here," she said. "Take Ronnie's until you are able to find one of your own. But be sure you come back next Sunday. We will save a place for you again."

"Thank you, Ma'am! I will try." The stranger put Ronnie's Bible in his pocket and hurried away.

That evening, Mrs. Walters prayed earnestly for the young stranger. "Oh Lord, please remember the young man who came to Thy house today. Teach him out of Thy Word and bring him to church again next Sunday."

But the next Sunday passed without any sign of the young man. After church Mother said, "Oh, Ronnie! I am so sad that he did not come! We must pray for him every day."

Another Sunday passed, and again Mother was disappointed. But on the third Sunday, the young man came to church again. Now he was neatly dressed, but he was very pale. Had he been ill?

As soon as the service was over, the young man laid Ronnie's Bible on the seat of their pew and quickly left. No one even had a chance to speak to him, and he never returned to church.

As Ronnie and his mother walked home from church, Mother turned the pages of the little Bible. On a blank page, she found a message from the stranger that said, *"Please remember me in your prayers."* The message was only signed with the initials *"H.B."*

Many years passed and Ronnie became

a man. He stayed with his mother and cared for her in her old age. Then one day his godly mother passed away, and Ronald was left alone. He now had to face the future on his own; he had to decide what to do. Ronald had always loved the sea, so he decided to be a doctor on a ship.

After many years of sailing, Ronald's ship was docked one weekend at a harbor in South Africa. When Sunday came, Ronald attended the service in a local church. After the service ended, a gentleman who had sat behind him leaned forward and said, "Excuse me, sir, but may I see your Bible a moment?"

Ronald handed him the Bible and watched as he quickly flipped through several pages. The gentleman then returned Ronald's Bible and followed him outside. As Ronald turned to go back to the ship, he felt a hand on his arm. "Please, sir! I must speak with you!"

Turning, Ronald found the same gentleman who had asked to borrow his Bible. "Why, certainly!" he answered. "Here is a bench. Let's just sit here for a while."

But instead of speaking, the gentleman sat studying Ronald's face. Then suddenly he bowed his head, and his whole body shook with great sobs. When he was able to speak again, he asked, "What is your name? Where are you from?"

When Ronald answered his questions, he continued, "Oh! I can't believe that we have met again after all these years, in a foreign land. Do you remember one time when you were a little boy that you invited a rough, mocking man to come to church with you?"

"Why, yes! I do remember! Are you the man my mother prayed for so many years?"

"I am so thankful to meet you again! I have often wanted to tell you the story of my life. You see, I also had Christian parents who gave me a Christian education. But my father died when I was only fifteen years old, so I had to quit school. I had to go to work to help support my mother.

"My mother was a very godly woman. She tried to teach me the fear of the Lord. But at my new job, I worked with many wicked men. I soon learned and was guilty of all sorts of sins, and that broke my poor mother's heart. After that I left the country to escape the law.

"I had stopped in Glasgow when you saw me. Seeing you as you were on your way to church with your mother that morning made me feel guilty. Then attending the service that morning brought to memory how I used to attend church with my mother. It made me remember how she used to pray for me, and especially when I broke her heart!"

At this point his voice broke and he could not go on for some time. At last he said with a shudder, "My dear mother! I have brought down her gray hairs with sorrow to the grave!"

Again he was overcome with grief, and tears flowed down his cheeks. "That service convicted me of guilt so severely that I became very ill for some time. It was on my sick bed that I came to know the Lord Jesus Christ as the heavenly Physician who could heal both body and soul. Your invitation that morning was used as the means that led to my conversion."

Ronald was filled with wonder and gratitude as he listened to this amazing story. He learned that Henry Bates, the rough looking man from long ago, was a missionary who had worked in South Africa now for many years.

"And do you remember the other rough man who was with me on that Sunday morning? He has been hanged for committing a terrible crime. Except for the grace of God, I would have been in that crime with him. I have been saved from the very brink of hell!"

As Henry finished his story, Ronald exclaimed, "When I remember how often my mother prayed for you, I see how beautifully God's Word has been fulfilled! 'Cast thy bread upon the waters, for thou shalt find it back after many days'" (Ecclesiastes 11:1).

Question: What was the cause of Henry's sickness and how was it cured?
Scripture reading: Ecclesiastes 11.

19. Robert's Revenge

Robert listened as his teacher read their memory text for the week. "'Therefore if thine enemy hunger, feed him; if he thirst, give him drink: for in so doing thou shalt heap coals of fire on his head.' This text can be found in Romans 12:20. Can anyone tell me what this means?"

Before anyone could raise a hand to answer, Robert clenched his fists and hissed, "No!"

"Excuse me, Robert," Mrs. Burns said, "Don't you understand the text?"

"Yes, I understand," he answered hotly, "but I will never do that!"

"See me after class, Robert. Perhaps then you can explain why you feel as you do."

Robert sat sullenly through the rest of the lesson. After class, he waited for Mrs. Burns. When everyone else had left, Mrs. Burns called Robert to her desk and said, "Now Robert, please explain why you behaved as you did during our Bible lesson."

"It's just not fair!" Robert burst out. "If you had an enemy like I have, you wouldn't be nice to him either. You would rather see him starve!"

"Why, Robert!" Mrs. Burns exclaimed. "How can you say such a thing? Whatever happened to make you feel so bitter?"

Anger burned in Robert's voice as he told Mrs. Burns his story. "Peter lives in the same apartment building as I do. He is always doing mean things to me. Yesterday just as I was coming home from school, he called to me from a window on the fourth floor. He had Jessie, my favorite cat, and threatened to throw her down. I screamed, 'No! Please don't hurt Jessie!' But he just laughed and threw her down anyway." Here Robert's voice broke with a sob and Mrs. Burn put her arm around his shaking shoulders.

"Did Jessie get hurt?" she asked.

"Oh, Mrs. Burns," he said through his tears "I picked her up and placed her in my own bed. I slept on the floor and kept checking her all night. But this morning, Jessie was dead! I had to find a place where I could bury her before school this morning."

"Oh, Robert!" Mrs. Burns tried to comfort him. "Peter did a very wicked thing, but yet our text for this week says that...."

"Never!" Robert interrupted. "Never would I help him! And even if I have to wait until I am a man, I will get even with him!" Before Mrs. Burns could try to reason with him, Robert ran from the room.

Robert ran outside only to find that it was raining and a cold wind was blowing. He decided to go home, even though no one would be home from work yet. He entered the apartment and passed the door where Peter and his father lived. Peter was home alone and his door was partly open. As Robert went by, Peter mockingly said, "Meeooow! Meeoow!"

Robert turned pale with anger. He put his hands over his ears and ran up to his apartment. He went to his own room and throwing himself across his bed, he muttered, "And we are supposed to give food to somebody like that if they are hungry? Never!" Robert fell asleep that night filled with thoughts of hatred for Peter.

The next morning as Robert hurried past Peter's door on his way to school, he heard someone crying. He stopped and cautiously approached the door. It was partly open so he looked into the room. There lay Peter on his bed with flushed cheeks, burning with fever. "Oh Robert," he groaned when he saw him standing in the doorway, "please call the landlady. My dad is gone and I feel so terrible. I need help!"

"Really? You feel terrible? Well, good! I'm glad to hear it!" Robert made an ugly face at Peter and left, closing Peter's door firmly so no one would hear him cry for help. Robert hurried off to school whistling happily. He hoped that Peter would be sick for a long time.

Robert was happier than usual all day. It didn't even bother him that he had to deliver his papers in the rain after school. He hurried through his route so he could go home, hoping that Peter was still sick. But going past Peter's door, Robert saw that a light was on and Mrs. Clark, the landlady, was with him. "Now Peter, just drink this and then maybe you can sleep for awhile," she was saying. "I need to go back to work or dinner will never be ready on time!"

Robert was sorry to see that Peter was being helped. But waiting until Mrs. Clark returned to the kitchen, he went to Peter's room. Leaning against the door frame, Robert asked, "Well, how are things going? Are you enjoying yourself now?" Robert was trying to sound mean, but Peter was too sick to notice. "Oh, Robert!" he groaned. "I am so full of pain, and I have such a bad headache. My head is burning like coals of fire." Hearing the words, "coals of fire," Robert turned pale. Fresh anger swept through him as he remembered the words of the text. Without saying another word, Robert ran back to his own room.

That night Robert went to bed as usual, but he could not sleep. In his mind he clearly pictured the words of the text over and over again: "Coals of fire," "coals of fire," "coals of fire." Everywhere he looked he seemed to see these words before his eyes. He could hear the hours passing; the clock in the church tower struck one o'clock. Finally he spoke aloud, "Okay, I will do it! I will do it!" He felt as though he were speaking to an invisible enemy.

Robert fell asleep immediately, but the next morning he remembered his promise. When he came to Peter's door, however, he saw that Peter's father was with him. "Good. Then I don't have to stop," he thought. With this excuse, Robert continued on his way to school. But everything seemed to go wrong that day. He could not keep his mind on his work. Robert hurried straight home to his room after school. Still thinking about the promise he had made, he finally decided he would keep it. He did not want to lie awake again tonight.

Peter's door was partly open when Robert went down. Peter was lying with his face to the wall. Robert went up to the bed and asked in a sharp tone, "Hey, Peter, do you need anything?" How he hated even speaking to Peter! But he was determined to keep his promise.

"I am so thirsty. They forgot to bring me some water." Peter's voice sounded very weak.

"Give him to drink!" muttered Robert as he got a glass of water. Then he grudgingly asked, "Are you hungry?"

Peter's answer was a terrible groan. Now Robert was faced with a problem. How could he keep the second part of the text? Leaving the room, he quickly walked to a nearby fruit market and asked to speak to the owner. "Sir, do you have any jobs that I could do for you?" he asked.

"Well, let me see. Yes, here's a fruit basket that needs to be delivered to this address."

"Thank you, sir." Robert took the basket and soon returned from delivering it. He did not get paid very much, but he used the money to buy a large, juicy orange. Returning to the apartment to Peter's room, Robert broke the orange into small cubes and helped Peter sit up to eat it. Peter's thankful expression made Robert uncomfortable. But he soon reminded himself that he was only feeding Peter because he had to. When Peter finished the orange, Robert jumped up to leave saying, "There! I fed you and gave you something to drink. Now I have done my duty!"

As Robert started to leave, Peter called out, "Please don't go yet. It's gets very lonely with nobody here."

"No way! That's not included in the text," Robert said and calmly left for the night, leaving a puzzled Peter behind. But Robert continued to do small jobs at the fruit market. For several nights he brought food and drink to Peter, but only because he felt he had to.

Then one evening when Robert came as usual, Peter suddenly asked, "Robert, do you think I will ever get better?"

"I don't know. What makes you ask such a question?"

"Dad asked the doctor to come, but after examining me, he just shook his head. I think I am going to die. Oh, Robert! I'm so afraid! And before I die, I want to tell you I'm sorry for what I did to your cat." Peter began to sob and the ice around Robert's heart melted.

"Aw, Peter, that's okay. Jessie was pretty old and probably would have died pretty soon anyway. Don't think about it anymore. But I hope you are not going to die! I will help take care of you as much as I can, Peter!"

That night Robert knelt beside his bed. He saw that the text was right. He must not try to get revenge. Now he could pray for Peter to recover. "Oh Lord," he prayed, "please help me to always do what the text says—but help me to do it from my heart. Please make Peter well again, and give us both a new heart."

How thankful Robert was to see that the Lord heard and answered his prayer! Three weeks later he was supporting a weak Peter as they went for a walk on a warm spring day. The boys soon felt as close as brothers. They began to sit in the sun, taking turns reading from the Bible. Both boys learned to search and value God's Word. They prayed that God would teach them to always obey His will.

Question: Did Robert lose out by obeying the command fom Scripture?
Scripture reading: Romans 12:3-21.

20. The Bold Little Bootblack

S

A little bootblack was standing near the entrance of a city hotel, waiting patiently for a job. Soon two fashionably dressed young men came out of the hotel, smoking their cigars, and stood near the boy.

"Here, Boots," said one of them, placing his foot on the boy's box of supplies. "Let's see if you are a master of your trade."

The bootblack scrubbed and polished the man's boot, doing his best to make it look like new. In the meantime, the young men were trying to frighten the little boy into working faster by swearing at him. The boy stood it as long as he could. But when one boot was finished, he stopped, and put his brushes back in the box.

"What are you doing?" cried the young men, exasperated.

"I won't finish your boots," answered the little boy boldly.

"What do you mean, not finish them!" exclaimed the young man with a dreadful oath. "Then you won't get your money!"

"I don't want your money," said the little boy. "I won't stay here and listen to your swearing."

"Leave the boy alone," said the other young man, "and let him finish his job."

"Alright," said the first man, "but it's a rare joke to find a bootblack who is afraid of swearing."

"Don't you know that swearing will cost you dearly?" exclaimed the boy.

"Do you mean to say that it costs something to swear?" asked the first young man in astonishment.

"Yes, sir," replied the little bootblack, in an earnest, solemn manner. "Without the cleansing blood of Jesus Christ swearing will cost you your soul."

Question: What does James 3:10 tell us about people who praise God one minute and curse the next?
Scripture reading: Acts 4:13-22.

21. The Little Girl and the Prisoner

A gentleman and his five-year-old daughter were walking hand in hand up and down the room at a railway station in England while waiting for a train. As they were waiting, two policemen came in, bringing with them a prisoner in chains. He was a very wicked man. He had just been sentenced to prison for twenty years. The policemen were taking him to the prison. They gave him a seat in a corner of the room. He was a mean-looking man, and everyone stayed away from him.

As the gentleman and his little girl walked up and down the room, the little girl could not keep her eyes off the prisoner. At first she was afraid of him, but when they reached the part of the room where he sat, she let go of her father's hand and went to the prisoner. In a gentle voice, and with her eyes full of tears, she said to him, "I feel sorry for you."

The prisoner frowned at her fiercely, and she ran back to her father's side. They continued their walk, and when they came near him again, she let go of her father's hand again, and spoke to the prisoner in the same tender tones, "The Lord Jesus is sorry for you, too."

Then the train came, and the girl and her father climbed aboard. The policemen and the prisoner boarded a different car, and the little girl never saw the prisoner again.

When the policemen reached the end of their journey, they delivered the prisoner to the keeper of the prison. "We are sorry to have to tell you this," said one of the policemen, "but this prisoner is ill-tempered and disobedient. He is very hard to manage, and we are afraid he will give you great trouble."

The keeper of the prison was worried. He had so many troublesome cases already, and he did not like having another one. He took extra precautions, making sure the prisoner could not escape and that he was never with any other prisoners.

But to the keeper's surprise, he had no trouble with this man. The prisoner did whatever he was told to do, and was always respectful and pleasant in his manner. The keeper did not know what to make of it. So, after a while he spoke to the prisoner and asked him how it was that he was so different from what he had been reported to be.

"Sir," answered the prisoner, "the report was true. I used to be as bad as possible, but now I am a changed man."

He went on to tell about what that dear child had said to him while waiting in the railway station. "Her sweet words melted my hard heart," he said. "They reminded me of my godly mother who is in heaven now. Her words led me to see what a sinner I was, and I turned in repentance to God. He heard my prayers. He gave me His pardon and peace in Christ. Now I am a new man and serve Jesus Christ."

The keeper was amazed. After some months, when he was convinced the prisoner had told him the truth, he allowed him to speak to the other prisoners. He proved to be a great blessing in that prison. The prisoner never forgot the little girl whose words were used to prick his conscience and bring him to Jesus.

Question: What did the little girl have in common with the prisoner's mother and why did it affect him so powerfully?
Scripture reading: 1 Timothy 1:12-17.

22. Tom's Trial

It was a pleasant day in summer when Tom and his dog, Tiger, walked slowly down the street together. Tom was thinking of all that had happened over the past year. It had been a difficult year, and one Tom would never forget. Nearly a year ago, on Tom's birthday, Tiger arrived as a present from Tom's uncle, who walked into the yard pulling a wagon with the dog in it. As soon as Tom saw the dog, he threw his arms around him. Tiger was pleased with his new master, and affectionately licked Tom's face. Within an hour they were close friends.

Tom had a bright, cheerful face, and if he were to stay at your home for a week, you would think him to be one of the nicest boys you ever knew. But some day you would discover that he had a bad temper. You would be alarmed to see his face turn red with anger as he stamped his feet, pushed his little sister, spoke rudely to his mother, and above all, displeased the Lord in heaven.

This story begins soon after Tiger and Tom became friends. It was summer vacation, and Tiger and Tom were walking down the street together when they met Richard

Casey, a boy in Tom's class at school.

"Richard!" called Tom. "I'm going to my dad's grain store for a while. Let's go up in the loft and play!"

Richard had just finished his work in his mother's garden, and was ready for a bit of fun. So the two went together to play in the loft of the big barn. They had great fun together for a while. But at last they began to argue over something one of the boys said. It was a foolish argument, not worth fighting over, but pretty soon there were angry words, and then, sad to say, Tom lost his temper. He punched and kicked Richard badly. Tiger, who seemed to be ashamed of his master, pulled hard at Tom's coat and whined, but in vain. At last Tom stopped, from mere exhaustion.

"Who's right now?" shouted Tom. "You or me?"

"I am!" sobbed Richard. "And you're lying!"

Tom lunged at Richard and gave him a hard shove. Richard stood near the open door of the loft. He screamed, threw up his arms, and a split second later, disappeared through the opening. Tom's heart stood still, and an icy chill crept over him. At first, he couldn't move, but then he flew down the stairs and made his way to Richard. Some men had heard Richard's scream and hurried to help. They bent over him anxiously.

"Is he dead?" Tom almost screamed.

"No," replied one of the men, "at least we hope not. How did he fall out?"

"He didn't fall," groaned Tom, white-faced. "I pushed him."

There was silence as everyone turned to look at Tom. "You pushed him? What were you thinking?" cried one of the men.

Tom hung his head miserably. He had no answer. The men quickly turned their attention to the unconscious boy. Some of the men scowled at him. A few moments later, Tom followed the crowd of people as they carried Richard into the store. He felt as though he were in a bad dream.

"Is he badly hurt?" someone asked.

"Only his hands," was the answer. "The rope saved him. He grabbed hold of it as he fell, but his hands are badly torn. He's passed out from the pain."

Just then Tom's father came in, and soon understood what had happened. The look he gave his unhappy son, so full of sorrow, not without pity, was too much for Tom. Tom quietly left the store, followed by the faithful Tiger. Together they wandered in the woods, and at last Tom threw himself on the ground. An hour ago he was a happy boy, playing with a school friend. And now—what a terrible change! What had caused this accident? Nothing but his wicked, violent temper. His mother had often warned him about his temper and the sad consequences it could bring. She had told him that little boys who do not learn to control their tempers will grow up to be ungodly men, and could possibly commit murder in a moment of violent anger. She had urged Tom to ask the Holy Spirit to renew his heart.

Now, Tom shuddered to think that he was almost a murderer! Nothing but God's great mercy, in putting that rope in Richard's way, had saved him from carrying that load of sorrow and guilt for the rest of his life. But poor Richard—he might still die! He looked so pale and still! Tom dropped to his knees and prayed God to spare Richard's life. With tears, he asked the Lord to forgive him, and to give him a new heart. He asked for God's help in trying to conquer his awful temper.

Tom could no longer bear the suspense—he just had to know how Richard was doing. So he went to Widow Casey's cottage. When he knocked at the door of the tiny house, Mrs. Casey angrily ordered him to leave.

"You've given me enough grief for a day," she scolded.

But Richard's feeble voice begged, "O mother, let him come in. I was just as bad as he was."

Tom was so glad to hear Richard's voice, that he hurried to his bedside. There lay poor Richard, with his hands bandaged, and looking very pale. But Tom was thankful that he was alive.

"I'm wondering how I'm going to make ends meet now," sighed Mrs. Casey, looking at her son. "Richard won't be able to help me like he used to. Who will weed the garden, and carry my vegetables to market? I'm afraid we won't have anything to eat when winter comes," and she covered her face with her apron.

"Mrs. Casey," said Tom eagerly, "I'll do everything that Richard did. I'll sell the potatoes and the beans, and I'll take Mr. Brown's cows to pasture every day and bring them home again."

Mrs. Casey shook her head in disbelief, but Tom kept his word. Every day Tom cared for Mr. Brown's cows, driving them to pasture early in the morning, and herding them back into the barn again in the evening. Widow Casey's garden was never kept in better order. And every morning, after the cows had been sent to the pasture, Tiger and Tom stood faithfully in the market place with the produce from Mrs. Casey's garden. They never gave up, no matter how warm the day became, until the last vegetable was sold. Faithfully, Tom placed the money in Mrs. Casey's hand when they returned.

Tom's father often passed through the village market, and he would give his son an encouraging smile, but he did not offer to help him out of his difficulty, for he knew if Tom struggled on alone, it would be a lesson he would never forget. Already, Tom was becoming more gentle and patient, and everyone noticed the change. His mother rejoiced over the sweet fruits of his repentance and self-sacrifice, and prayed they would continue.

After a few weeks, the bandages were removed from Richard's hands. The village did not have a skilled doctor, so Richard had not received the treatment he should have. Now his hands were misshapen and pulled together in a strange manner. Mrs. Casey could not hide her disappointment.

"He will never be the help he was before," she wept. "He will never be like other boys. He had such fine handwriting, and now he can barely write at all!"

"If we only had a good doctor like they have in the cities," sighed a neighbor. "Even now, his hands might be helped if you took him to New York."

"But I'm too poor! I'll never be able to pay for a good doctor's services!" cried Mrs. Casey, and she burst into tears.

Tom could not bear to see her weep, so he rushed off into the woods to think. He had no money to give; he had already given his small allowance to Widow Casey. All at once, a thought flashed into Tom's head, and he stopped walking. But he shook his head, saying, "No, no! I just can't do that!"

Tiger gently licked his hands, and watched him with concern. Now came a great struggle. Tom stroked Tiger while he cried. Tiger whined, licked his face, rushed off into dark corners, and barked savagely at some imaginary enemy, then came back, and putting his paws on Tom's knees, wagged his tail in anxious sympathy. At last Tom took his hands from his pale, tear-stained face, and looking into the dog's great trusting eyes, he said in a shaky voice, "Tiger, old boy! Dear old dog, could you ever forgive me if I sold you?"

Then came more tears, and Tom got up quickly, as if afraid he would change his mind, and almost ran out of the woods. Over the fields he raced, with Tiger close at his heels, nor rested a moment till he stood at Major White's door, nearly two miles away.

When the Major opened the door, Tom asked, panting, "Do you still want to buy Tiger, sir?"

"Why, yes, I'd love to," answered the old man in great surprise, "but do you want to sell him?"

"Yes, please," gasped Tom, not daring to look at the old man.

The exchange was quickly made, and the money placed in Tom's hand. Tom led Tiger into Major White's barn, quickly closed the door, and turned to leave. In a choking voice he called out, "You'll be kind to him, Major White, won't you? Don't whip him! I never did. He's the best dog...."

"No, no, child," said Major White kindly. "I'll treat him like a prince, and if you ever want to buy him back, you shall have him."

Tom managed to falter, "Thank you," and almost flew out of hearing of Tiger's frantic scratching on the barn door.

Tom's money was gladly accepted by the Widow Casey, and arrangements were made to take Richard to New York City. A friend took the boy to the city free of charge, and Tom's money was enough to cover the operation. The crooked fingers were corrected, and soon they were almost as good as ever. The whole village loved Tom for his brave, self-sacrificing spirit, and for what he had done to make up for the consequences of his bad temper.

A few days after Richard's return came Tom's birthday, but Tom was not feeling very happy. In spite of his great joy in Richard's recovery, he mourned the loss of his friend Tiger. Since it was Tom's birthday, he was allowed to spend the day as he pleased, so he took some books and went to his favorite place in the woods.

"How different from my last birthday," thought Tom. "Then I had just gotten Tiger, and I was so happy, although I love him more now than I did that day."

Tom sighed, but thought more cheerfully, "But I hope some things are better now than they were last year. I have learned how important it is to have a new heart. I hope I have begun to conquer my bad temper, and with God's help, I will never give up trying as long as I live. I do wish, though, that I had enough money to buy back dear old Tiger. I'm not sorry, though, that I sold him to help Richard."

While Tom was busy with his thoughts,

he heard a hasty, familiar trot, a quick bark of joy, and the brave, friendly dog sprang into Tom's arms.

"Tiger!" cried Tom, trying to sound angry, although he couldn't hold back his tears, "you naughty dog! Why did you run away?"

Tiger responded by picking up a letter he had dropped in his first bark of joy, and laid it in Tom's lap. Quickly Tom tore it open.

My dear child,

Tiger is pining for his beloved master, and I must do what's best for him. I want him to have a good master, and, knowing that the best masters are those who have learned to govern themselves, I send him to you. Will you take care of him, and make me happy?

Your old friend,
Major White

P. S. I know the whole story. Dear young friend, "Be not weary in well-doing" (2 Thessalonians 3:13).

Tom read the words through a mist of tears. He hugged the dog, and gave thanks to God, not only for giving him his beloved dog back, but for teaching him a lesson he would never forget.

Question: How was Tom different the second time that Tiger appeared on his birthday?
Scripture reading: Genesis 4:1-15.

23. William, the African Slave

A young boy was wandering on a beautiful African coast, studying the sandy beach. Every few steps, he would stoop down to pick up a shell. If he thought it worth keeping, he would add it to his growing collection in the hand-woven basket he carried. He stretched and looked at the sun to tell him the time. Then he looked farther down the beach and stared in amazement. Some white sailors were approaching him. He had never seen white people before, and he watched them with open curiosity.

Suddenly the men rushed toward him. The boy dropped his basket and fled. But the sailors were quicker than he was and they soon caught him. He screamed and shouted for his father and mother, but the sailors were strong, and easily carried the struggling child onto their ship. As they pushed him down into the hold (the bottom level) of the ship, a dreadful smell filled his nostrils. It was so dark! At first the boy couldn't see anything. He heard groans, and chains rattling. Then suddenly the boy screamed. They were people who were groaning, who were in chains!

One of the sailors slapped him and shouted something in a language the boy did not understand. Roughly, the sailor shoved the boy onto a narrow plank and clamped cold iron shackles around his ankles. Too terrified to make a sound, the little boy lay motionless, staring hopelessly at the plank above him, just inches away from his face.

On the seemingly endless voyage, many prisoners died and most became ill. The little boy also became ill, but recovered. He was still very weak when the ship arrived in Jamaica. The slaves were herded into a market square and auctioned off. The little boy also was sold.

The boy's owner and his wife named him William. They treated him well enough, but William desperately missed his dear father and mother. William's fears and loneliness soon turned to bitterness. He told himself that all white people were evil spirits and would pay for what they had done to him, so he stole food when he worked in the kitchen. He did his duties as they were required of him, but with hatred and bitterness in his heart.

Several years passed. Then one evening William was summoned by his master.

"William," stated his owner, "you will go with Captain Wells. He is your new owner."

William was filled with fear. Would his new master be cruel? Would he have to go on that terrible ship again? After all, the man was a captain!

William was greatly relieved to discover that he was to be the personal servant of Captain Wells on his voyage to America. He slept in a tiny room beside the Captain's cabin. His work was not difficult. Life on the upper decks of a ship was certainly better than in the hold! With a shudder William thought of those terrible weeks in the bottom of the slave-ship. He swore he would never like or trust any white man.

Although Captain Wells was not a church-going man, he considered himself a Christian. He was a kind-hearted man; he appeared to keep God's commandments. William considered himself fortunate to have gotten such a good master.

They were in America for only a month. The Captain had business to take care of, and often William was free to do as he liked while the Captain had meetings.

One evening, while Captain Wells was having dinner at the home of one of his friends, William wandered down the streets. He noticed that many people were heading toward the edge of town. Being curious, he followed. In the distance, he could see a large crowd of people. A man was on a platform. William was soon close enough to hear what he was saying. From the very beginning, it seemed to William that the minister spoke to him alone. He spoke about sin — how it lives in each of us, in our thoughts and deeds. "And God saw that the wickedness of man was great in the earth, and that every imagination of the thoughts of his heart was only evil continually" (Genesis 6:5).

"How does this man know so much about me?" wondered William.

William was deeply convicted. He saw that his lying, stealing, hatred, and bitterness were all terrible sins against a holy and just God. He felt the minister was speaking only about him, for surely no one else was such a wicked sinner as he!

But the minister had more to say. He spoke about the love of Jesus Christ for undeserving sinners. Once again, it seemed the minister looked only at William as he said, "Jesus Christ came to die for sinners, black sinners as well as white sinners."

William's tears fell fast, for he felt that he did not deserve Christ's love. How he wanted to love Jesus, but he felt he did not know how, and that made William very sad.

Thoughtfully he made his way back to his little room. There he folded his hands and closed his eyes as he had seen the minister do. "Jesus," said William, "I heard a good minister today. I am a very wicked sinner. I knew nothing, I did not believe in Thee. My thoughts and actions are not good. Jesus Christ died for wicked sinners. This is very good, very good indeed, to do for wicked sinners. I must love Jesus Christ, but I do not know how! My heart seems hard like a stone. I want to love Jesus Christ! Amen."

Three more times, William went to hear the "good minister." William had no one to talk to, but he told everything to God. "Dear God," he would say, "the good minister says that God hears the cry of the poor, so I cry to Thee." And God heard William, and made Himself precious to him.

Soon it was time for Captain Wells to return to his wife and children in England. On the voyage the Captain gave William a Bible. But he couldn't read! So he asked a sailor to teach him. The sailor taught William the letters of the alphabet, but had neither the time nor patience to teach him more. With childlike faith, William asked God to teach him to read. So, with the desire to read God's Word, and with many prayers to God for help, William learned to read.

During every spare moment he could find, William read his Bible. He read all about Jesus Christ, how He loves sinners, how wicked men killed Him, how He died and rose again. This made William weep, to think that Jesus did all that for him!

The sailors on the ship noticed William's interest in the Bible. Some laughed at him, some ignored him, one or two respected him, and some called him names. William talked to God constantly in his heart. "Lord Jesus," he prayed, "some sailors who do not love Thee call me a great fool, negro dog, and black hypocrite. And that makes me feel angry. But then I remember Christians must not be angry. Thou wast called ugly, black names, and Thou wast quiet as a lamb; and so then I remember Thee, Jesus, and I say nothing again to them. Jesus said little and prayed much. And so then I say nothing at all."

When they landed safely in England, Captain Wells bought a house in a little village. William went with the family, and was kept very busy helping them unpack and move in. William had seen a church in the village on the way to their new home, and longed to attend the services, but he was kept so busy that there was no way for him to go.

After the family had settled in, they entertained friends and family. William worked in the kitchen, and it seemed there was no end to the work. But while he worked, he talked to the other servants about the great love of Jesus Christ who had come to die for wicked sinners. Often he was teased and laughed at for taking religion so seriously. When he sighed one Sunday and said he would love to go to church, a maid laughed, "Church? Stop dreamin', lad! There's work to be done, and plenty of it!"

But God knew William's desire; He made a way for him to go to church. The Wells family was invited to spend some time with friends, so they packed their trunks and went to visit for a few days. That left very little to do in the kitchen, so, on Sunday morning William went to church.

William drank in every word the minister said. Reverend Richmond preached about the Philippian jailer who believed and was baptized. William wished to be baptized and belong to a church of Jesus Christ!

When the family returned, William asked the Captain if he could be baptized, and go to church every Sunday. His heart pounded. What if the Captain forbade it?

"It won't hurt," he said, "but Cook will expect you to do your chores before you leave. You must get up very early, William."

"Yes, master, I will be glad to do that," smiled William eagerly. "Master, if it's no trouble, could you please ask the minister if he would be willing to baptize me?"

"Does it mean that much to you?" asked the Captain, a little surprised.

"Yes, master, I very much wish to be a Christian," said William earnestly.

"Well, you are a very good servant to me, William. I will speak to Reverend Richmond tomorrow when I go into the village."

"Oh thank you, sir, thank you," cried William. "And I thank Thee, Lord," he added in a whisper.

The Captain did speak to the pastor, and arranged for William to meet with him the following afternoon. Reverend Richmond was happy to visit with William. He asked William many questions, and thus found out his story. The minister was delighted at the simple, sincere faith of this young African.

A few days later Reverend Richmond set out to visit William at the Wells's home. The road wound its way along the coast. It was a beautiful sight. The pastor got off his horse and walked to the edge of the chalk cliff. Looking down, he could see the waves wash up on the rocky shore. Puffins flew below him, in and out of the nests they had built in the holes of the cliff. Over to his left, on one of the huge rocks below him, Reverend Richmond noticed someone sitting, with a book in his hand. The pastor smiled. It was his African friend. Carefully he descended the cliff by way of a crudely built staircase which had been cut into the rock by fishermen and shepherd boys.

William didn't notice the minister until he was almost beside him.

"Pastor! I am very glad to see you!"

"I am glad to see you reading your Bible. It is a good sign," observed the minister, sitting down beside William.

"Yes, master, it is a sign that God is good to me, but I am never good to God."

"How so?" asked the minister.

"I never thank Him enough who gave me all these good things. I am afraid my heart is very bad. I think there is nobody like me, nobody feels such a heart as mine."

"William," explained the minister, "your feelings are like those of every true believer who feels the great sinfulness of sin and the greatness of the price which Christ Jesus paid. You can say in the words of the

116

hymn: *I, the chief of sinners am, but Jesus died for me.*

"Oh yes, sir, I believe that Jesus died for me. What would become of a wicked sinner, if Christ did not die for him? But He died for the chief of sinners, and that makes my heart quite glad."

"What part of the Bible were you just reading, William?"

"I read how the man on the Cross spoke to Christ, and Christ spoke to him. Now that man's prayer will just do for me, 'Lord, remember me.' 'Lord, remember this sinner' — this is my prayer every morning and sometimes at night too. When I cannot think of many words, then I say again 'Lord, remember this sinner.'"

"And be assured, William, the Lord hears that prayer. He will not cast out any that come to Him."

"I believe that, sir, but there is so much sin in my heart; it makes me afraid and sorry. Do you see how these limpets and shellfish cling very tightly to the rocks? Just so, sin sticks fast to my heart."

"It may be so, William," answered the pastor, "but think about this: If you belong to Jesus Christ, then just as these limpets cling to these rocks, neither seas nor storms shall separate you from His love."

"Oh, that is just what I want!" cried William, with tears in his eyes. "I would give all this world, if I had it, to be without sin and cling to Jesus!"

"Come then, and welcome to Jesus Christ, my brother," said Reverend Richmond gently. "His blood cleanses from all sin. He gave Himself a ransom for sinners. 'Surely he hath borne our griefs, and carried our sorrows: yet we did esteem him stricken, smitten of God, and afflicted. But he was wounded for our transgressions, he was bruised for our iniquities: the chastisement of our peace was upon him; and with his stripes we are healed' (Isa. 53:4-5). Come, freely come to Jesus, the Savior of sinners."

"Yes, pastor," answered William, weeping, "I will come, but I am coming very slowly, very slowly. I want to run, I want to fly to Jesus! Jesus is very good to me, to send you to tell me all this."

When it was time to go, Reverend Richmond asked William if he would like to join a group of Christian friends on Wednesday evening for Bible study and prayer. William, of course, said he would like it very much.

But when Wednesday evening came, William, who was walking with Reverend Richmond, was not sure he should go after all. "Pastor, I am not good enough to be with such good people. I am a great sinner. They are good Christians."

"If you were to ask them, William," smiled the minister, "they would each tell you they were worse than anybody. You will only meet a group of poor fellow sinners who love to speak of and sing the praises of redeeming love. And I am sure that is a song you would like to sing, too!"

"Oh yes, that song is very good for me!"

The little group of people warmly welcomed William. Each one had a kind word for him.

"Pastor," said William with tears in his eyes, "I do not know what to say to these good friends. I think this looks like a little heaven upon earth."

Toward the end of the evening, the pastor explained that William wished to be baptized, and that he would like to ask William some questions to show whether or not he was ready to be baptized. Reverend Richmond asked him many questions, beginning with simple ones, then more difficult ones.

"What is it to have faith?"

"I suppose," answered William thoughtfully, "that it is to think often about Jesus Christ; to love Him very much, to believe all He says to be true, to pray to Him very much, and when I feel very weak and sinful, to think that He is very strong and good—and that it is all for my sake."

"And do you feel you have this faith?"

"Oh, pastor, I think sometimes I have no faith at all!"

"Why so, William?"

"When I want to think about Jesus Christ, my mind runs after other things, and when I want to love Him, my heart seems quite cold. When I want to believe all that He says to sinners is true, then I think it is not true for me. When I want to pray, the devil puts bad thoughts into me, and I never thank Christ enough. Now all this makes me sometimes afraid I have no faith."

"I think," smiled Reverend Richmond, "that I can prove that you do have faith. Did you, by your own self, begin to think of yourself as a great sinner and to feel your need of a Savior?"

"Oh no! It came when I thought nothing about it, and did nothing about it. The good God did it; I could not do it myself, I am sure of that!"

"Do you think that Jesus Christ and His salvation is most desirable?"

"Oh yes!"

"Do you believe He is able to save you?"

"Yes, He is able to save completely and forever."

"Do you think He is unwilling to save you?"

"I dare not say that. He so good, so merciful, so kind, to say He will not cast out any that come to Him."

"Do you wish, and desire, and strive to keep His commandments?"

"Yes, pastor, because I love Him, and that makes me want to do as He says."

"Are you willing to suffer for His sake, if God should call you to do so?"

"I think I could die for the love of Him! He did not think it too much to die for me. Why should a wicked sinner think it too much to die for so good and righteous a Savior?"

The people in the room were much moved by William's clear and deep love for Jesus.

"I think, William, thy faith hath made thee whole." said Reverend Richmond and with that they closed the evening with praise to God, singing this song:

See, a stranger comes to view,
Though he's black,* he's comely too.
Come to join the choirs above,
Singing of redeeming love.

Welcome, dear friend, welcome here,
Banish doubt, and banish fear.
You, who Christ's salvation prove,
Praise and bless redeeming love.

On Sunday, William was baptized. It was a day he never forgot. Not long afterward he went with Captain Wells on another voyage. Reverend Richmond never saw him again, and often wondered what happened to him, but he always prayed for this dear brother in Christ who had been saved in such a remarkable way.

Question: How did William know that Christ was willing to save him?
Scripture reading: Romans 8:31-39.

*Song of Solomon 1:5

24. Trust in the Lord

Looking up anxiously at his mother, Bobby pleaded earnestly. "Don't cry, Mommy."

"Bobby, we are in trouble," answered his mother. "Daddy has left us, and he said he'll never come back!"

Mrs. Smith's tears fell over the baby she was nursing. She had five children younger than Bobby, who was eight. Their father, who had been out of work for some time, had just deserted them. What was she to do? They were so poor! Who would look after them?

"Mommy," said Bobby, "that's very bad news, but God knows our trouble. He will help us when we pray to Him. I heard a Bible story about God helping a poor widow with her boys."

"But He doesn't love me, Bobby," sighed his mother. "I'm not as good as I ought to be, and I've not thought much about Him. No, He doesn't love me," she finished sadly.

"The Lord is so good. He has been good to us all the time!" answered Bobby eagerly. "When Emmie is naughty and stays out playing instead of coming in to bed when you call—you still love her, don't you?"

"Yes, but that's different," said Mrs. Smith, "and you'll see He won't help me now when I'm in such trouble."

"He will if we ask Him!" cried Bobby confidently. "It's in the Bible! We learned it in Sunday School. 'Ask, and it shall be given you. If ye then, being evil, know how to give good gifts unto your children, how much more shall your Father which is in heaven give good things to them that ask Him?' Mother, let's ask Him right now."

"Well, all right," said Mrs. Smith, wiping her eyes on her apron.

Calling his brothers and sisters together, Bobby made them all kneel down with clasped hands. Then he and his mother knelt too. "Now, Mother, pray," Bobby whispered. But Mrs. Smith could not say a word. She felt as if there were a great lump in her throat. It was long ago that she had tried to pray.

So Bobby prayed. "God, Daddy's left us. Make him come home. Help me and Mommy to earn money and get food for the children, for Jesus' sake. Amen."

Mrs. Smith and the children said, "Amen," and the children jumped up, eager to do something else. Bobby rose too, looking very serious. "Mommy," he said, "my teacher says we must do our best and work hard. I must work as well as pray."

"But Bobby, what could you do?" asked his mother.

"I can sell matchboxes or newspapers," he answered eagerly.

"The streets?" exclaimed Mrs. Smith, "oh my boy, I've always tried to keep you off of the streets!"

"God is everywhere, Mommy. Isn't He in the streets, too?" asked Bobby, wonderingly.

"Yes, of course He is. Well, we have no choice, so you must work in the streets. I have just two coins left, Bobby. You may take one and see what you can do." Mrs. Smith sighed in helpless frustration as she watched her young son set out to look for work.

Bobby, on the other hand, was delighted. A friend of his sold newspapers, and could make forty-four cents in one night by selling newspapers in the streets.

Bobby had a clear voice, and it seemed to carry everywhere as he walked proudly along, singing out the name of the newspaper like the other newsboys. Evening after evening he earned money in this way for his mother.

Each evening, before leaving for work, Bobby gathered his mother, brothers, and sisters around him. He would read the Bible and recite the texts he had learned in Sunday School. Then he would ask God for His help and protection. He also prayed that God would save their father and return him to them.

All went well until one evening, when the rain came down in torrents. Mrs. Smith wanted to keep Bobby home, but she desperately needed the money so she reluctantly let him go out.

He came back soaked and chilled. Mrs. Smith hurried him to bed. He became very hot, and mumbled in his sleep. The next day he was worse, and could not even lift his head from the pillow. The following night his mother sat up with him, for he seemed barely conscious.

During the long, quiet night, Mrs. Smith thought about the stories and texts Bobby had learned in his Sunday School classes, and she prayed to the great heavenly doctor to heal her boy and return him to her.

In the early morning Bobby opened his eyes, and recognized his mother. But his first words were, "Mommy, do I hear Daddy?"

Mrs. Smith looked up in amazement to see her husband entering the room.

"Hester," he said to his wife. "I'm very sorry I've been such a bad husband to you. But I'm a changed man now, by the grace of God. And what's more, I've found a very good job, thanks be to God. But what's this? Is Bobby ill?"

"Bobby will get well now," exclaimed Mrs. Smith. "Let's thank God for it."

Husband and wife knelt together beside Bobby's bed, and with trembling voices thanked Him for His goodness.

Question: Can you think of a Bible story which tells us about God helping a widow and her son?
Scripture reading: 2 Kings 4:1-7.

126

25. Whiter Than Snow

In one of the beautiful palaces of England, there lived a nobleman who was not a Christian and who never went to church. He had a lovely little girl about six years old. Her name was Alberta. She was the delight of her father's heart.

One day she was alone with him in the library, playing, while he did some paperwork. Suddenly she stopped playing, got up and stood beside her father. Looking earnestly into his face, she asked, "Daddy, do you know anything whiter than snow?"

"No, my darling," he answered, smiling, "there isn't anything whiter than snow."

"Oh, yes there is!" exclaimed Alberta.

"And what would that be?" asked her father, laying down his pen and taking her little hands in his.

"Daddy, the soul washed in the blood of the Lord Jesus is whiter than snow!"

The nobleman was surprised and very displeased at this answer. He had never taught his child about religion, and did not want anyone else to teach it to her either.

"Who taught you that, my child?" he asked, trying to keep the anger out of his voice.

"My nurse, Mary, did," she answered. When Alberta saw her father's stern look, she asked, "Are you angry with me, Daddy?"

"No, I am not angry with you, my dear. I just don't want you to learn all this nonsense. Mary will have to leave us."

No matter how hard Alberta cried and pleaded, the nobleman's mind was made up. He rang a bell, and a servant appeared. "Tell Mary to come at once," he ordered.

The nurse came to the library.

"Tell me, Mary," he demanded, "have you been teaching my child about Jesus?"

"Yes sir, I have," she replied.

"I cannot allow you to teach my child such things," he exclaimed. "Go to the steward and get the wages due to you, and then leave the castle within the hour."

"Yes sir, I will leave as you ask, but I will pray for you and your daughter every day," answered Mary quietly. Then she hugged Alberta tightly and left the library.

Not long after this, a royal prince came to spend a few days with the nobleman. Everyone in the castle felt honored to have the prince visit their castle, and did their best to give the prince the best hospitality.

One day during this visit, the prince was sitting with the nobleman in his library. Alberta was there too, playing with her doll. The prince called her to him, and taking her on his knee, he chatted with her, telling her he missed his own children at home. Then she looked at him with her soft brown eyes, and asked, "Prince, do you know anything that is whiter than snow?"

"No dear," he answered kindly, "I have never heard of anything that is whiter than snow. Have you?"

"Oh yes, Prince! The soul that is washed from its sins in the blood of Jesus Christ is whiter than snow."

There was silence in the library after this. Neither the prince nor the nobleman had a word to say. But these words had a strange effect on Alberta's father. Suddenly, all his riches lost their glitter. His life seemed very empty. A tiny spark of longing to be cleansed flickered in his heart and when he found a Bible he began to read it and he began to pray. He also felt bad for sending Mary away. He wrote her a letter, asking her to return. He also told her that she must talk not only with the child, but also himself, about the blood of Jesus Christ.

How happy Mary was! How she had prayed for this! Joyfully, she returned to the castle; prayerfully, she returned to her work. Together, the nobleman, his daughter, and Mary sought God's mercy and found it. They found it to be true that the soul that has been washed in the blood of Jesus is whiter and more beautiful than snow.

Question: How did Mary know that the soul that is washed in the blood of Jesus is whiter than the snow?
Scripture reading: Hebrews 9:16-21.

26. Willie

William James Carpenter was a cheerful child, always eager to please his parents, and very tender in his feelings. A touching story told or read to him would bring tears to his eyes. When he did something wrong, his parents would gently correct him on the basis of God's Word, and this would also make him cry. He was an honest boy as well.

Willie liked to read the morning portion of Scripture after breakfast. One morning, his father returned home and, noticing that both Willie and his mother had been crying, asked what was wrong. Mrs. Carpenter answered, "Willie said a bad word this morning and that has made me very sad. I've told Willie that God hears all that we say, and He sees all that we do. He heard what Willie said and it has displeased Him."

Seeing his mother in tears was too much for Willie, and he also had burst into tears.

Mr. Carpenter said little as he ate his breakfast. After he had finished, he said to Willie, "Willie, I'd like you to read Proverbs, chapter four. Start reading at verse fourteen."

Willie began reading: "Enter not into the path of the wicked, and go not in the way of evil men. Avoid it, pass not by it, turn from it, and pass away."

As he read, his father pointed out the difference between the people of God and the wicked, and the sad result of associating with worldly companions, and so learning their bad words and ways.

When Willie came to the twenty-fourth verse, his voice faltered, "Put away from thee a froward mouth, and perverse lips put far from thee." He read a few words more before he broke down and sobbed, so that he could not go on. At last he said, "You finish reading, Daddy. I can't."

God made His own Word a rod to him, which had far better results than any punishment his father could have given him. Willie never used that word again or any other word like it.

Some time in June of 1903, diphtheria broke out among the children in Willie's neighborhood. Several were taken to the hospital, and some of them died.

Willie seemed to be healthy, and played happily with his friends. But one night in July he became restless, complaining of a headache. He had a fever, so his mother kept him in bed the following day. Mr. Carpenter tried to assure his wife that in a few days Willie would be better. But on Sunday, Willie began to complain about a sore throat. This frightened Mrs. Carpenter, since that was an indication of diphtheria. She immediately sent for the doctor. After the doctor had examined Willie, he gravely stated that Willie had diphtheria in the worst form, and was to be taken to the hospital as soon as possible.

Willie was willing to go, but some time later he became worried. He asked his mother to read Psalms 23 and 24. Then she prayed aloud with him. Willie whispered, "Mommy, tell Daddy to pray for me, too."

Mr. Carpenter was very much surprised to find Willie so sick. But he did not think for a moment that his son would die. He did feel, however, that it was a time for earnest prayer.

Shortly before Willie left for the hospital, his father sat by Willie's bedside. Willie looked very sad. When Mr. Carpenter asked him, "Do you want us to pray for you?" Willie answered, "Yes."

Mr. Carpenter then informed him, "You know, my dear boy, that neither Mommy's nor Daddy's prayers will take you to heaven. You must pray yourself. Try to ask God to teach you to pray. Jesus is the good and wise Doctor. He is the skillful Physician. He alone can make you better. Ask Him to bless you and give you a new heart."

The boy thought much about his father's words. During the week, one of the nurses asked him if he prayed. He answered simply, "I try to do what my daddy told me."

Although the doctor did all he could to help Willie, the boy steadily grew worse.

On Saturday morning, Mrs. Carpenter received a message that she and her husband were to come at once if they wanted to see Willie alive. When they arrived at the hospital, they saw that he was indeed very ill and deathly pale. He smiled when he saw his parents. He seemed sad, and at the same time very loving, as he saw how pained his father and mother were to see him suffer. It was a very moving scene. Even the nurses brushed away tears, for they all loved this quiet, thoughtful boy.

Willie asked his parents to pray for him, adding that he had been trying to pray for himself. During the night one of the nurses had heard him trying to sing, telling her that he had a hope that he would be with Jesus.

All that afternoon and night, Mr. and Mrs. Carpenter stayed with Willie. Sunday morning his condition worsened, and the doctor agreed that they should not leave him. How his parents prayed and wept before the Lord, begging Him to hear their cries, and work graciously in the heart of their dear son! They had a good hope that he was one of the Lord's little ones, but they wanted to see more evidences of a real change. So they went on pleading, "Lord, bless him. Forgive his sins. Make it clear to him and to us that he is one of Thy children. Enable him to leave a dying testimony. Help and sustain him in the agonies of death. Dear Lord, incline Thy ear and answer our requests. Thou art able.

Willie is not too young. We ask this for Jesus' sake. Amen."

His parents suffered with Willie as he moaned in pain. It was clear that the end was drawing near. Once his father asked him, "Willie, do you think you will go to heaven when you die?"

"I hope so," answered Willie.

"Why do you hope so?" probed his father.

Willie made no reply, but his look was earnest and full of meaning. Mr. Carpenter could only encourage him to keep praying to Jesus. "He alone can make you ready to die. He hears little children when they really pray. Keep on praying, Willie dear. Ask Jesus to bless you and give you to feel that you are one of His lambs whom He is about to take to His heavenly fold."

Much as his father loved him, he did not dare to put his son at ease too soon. Willie's father wanted to wait for the Lord Himself to work faith in his heart. Both parents knew that Willie must be born again in order to see the kingdom of God. That is the work of grace which God alone can do, also in the heart of a ten-year-old boy.

Early Tuesday morning, July 20, Mr. and Mrs. Carpenter sat at Willie's bedside once more. His cries of pain indicated that death was doing its work. His parents begged God, if it were His will, to shine on Willie in grace and mercy, and take him to Himself. They asked Him to make it plain that it really was God's own work in Willie's heart.

Mrs. Carpenter left the room occasionally, for she could not bear to see her child suffer. Willie would often say, "I just can't sleep." After a while he turned onto his left side and lay quietly. Noticing that his mother was gone, he anxiously called out for her. She was at his side in an instant. Then he tried to sing:

> Guide me, O Thou great Jehovah,
> Pilgrim through this barren land.
> I am weak, but Thou art mighty,
> Hold me with Thy powerful hand.
> Bread of Heaven, Bread of Heaven,
> Feed me till I want no more;
> Feed me till I want no more.

It was very indistinct. He turned over on his other side, and then, with all the strength he had left, uttered a cry of victory in a clear voice: "Alleluia!" A few more struggles and feeble breathings, and his life was ended. His spirit had been taken by the angels to God the Father's house of many mansions. There in heaven he was among the many people who were washed in the blood of Christ, saved by Him from sin. It was remarkable that, at the same time that he died, the congregation at the church was praying on his behalf. So God heard and answered the prayers of the congregation as well as those of his parents.

Tears filled their eyes now. The nurses could not help weeping either as they heard his dying words and watched him draw his last breath. Willie's parents were filled with love for their child, but also with gratitude to God for granting them a clear sign of His work. They now felt confident of Willie's eternal safety, and were able to praise the name of the Lord. He had, in the words of David, "heard the voice of their supplications and inclined his ear unto them" (Psalm 116:1-2).

Question: Who did Willie need to make him ready to die? According to Numbers 6:22-26, who gives us peace? What encouragement does Job 19:25-27 give to Christians when facing death?
Scripture reading: 1 Samuel 3:1-10.

27. The Little Chimney Sweep's Prayer

Some children in a Sunday school class had to work so hard during the week that they were sometimes forgetting to pray. Ten-year-old Peter had to work very hard as a chimney sweep so his teacher asked him, "Peter, do you ever pray?"

"Oh yes, sir!" he replied.

"And when do you do this? You go out very early every morning, don't you?"

"Well I'm only half awake when we leave the house. I think about God, but I cannot say that I pray then. You see, our master orders us to climb the chimney quickly, but we are allowed to rest a little at the top. Then I sit on the chimney top and pray."

"And what do you pray?"

"Very little. I don't know beautiful words with which to speak to God. Usually I only repeat a verse that I have learned at school."

"What is that?"

Peter answered very earnestly, "God be merciful to me a sinner."

Question: Is the prayer of the publican also your prayer? Pray that God may make it so in truth.

Scripture reading: Luke 18:9-14.

Prayer Points

God's Care

1. ★ Pray to God for the spiritual encouragement of those who preach God's Word. Ask God to protect them from sin and temptation.

   ❧ Pray to God that you will listen to God's Word when preached as it is Christ's message of love to sinners. Ask God to open your ears and your heart to Him.

2. ★ Thank God for the provision of food and drink. Thank Him that He knows what it is like to be human and that when He was on the cross He was thirsty and suffered so much for sinners.

   ❧ Ask God to give you a hunger and thirst for Him. Pray that instead of yearning for things and possessions, you will long to know Him.

3. ★ Thank Jesus Christ for how He loves to save sinners and that He longs to shelter His people and protect them like a chicken protects her baby chickens under her wings.

   ❧ Pray that God will teach you the danger of sin and of a life without Christ. Ask Him to lead you away from danger and to take you to Himself.

4. ★ Ask God to make you willing to do even difficult things for Him and to stand up for God against persecution.

   ❧ Thank Jesus Christ that He was willing to die for His elect and that He became sin for sinners even when He had never sinned. Ask Him to take away your sins and turn you from evil ways.

5.　★ Make your requests known to God. Share your anxieties with Him and thank Him for His love and power to help in times of need.

❖ Thank God that He listens to sinners and can give you everything you need. Ask Him to show you your greatest needs of salvation and freedom from sin.

6.　★ Thank God for missionaries who are teaching people who have not heard the wonderful news of Jesus Christ. Pray that more missionaries and pastors will be called by God to work for Him.

❖ Ask God to help you to conquer your doubts. Bring your needs and requests to the one powerful God. Ask Him to make you grow up to be a man or woman of God and to wash you from your sin in Christ's blood.

7.　★ Tell God how amazing He is. Praise His name for all He has done for your soul.

❖ Ask God to protect you from sinning and misusing His holy name. Ask God to make His name the most honored in your life.

8.　★ Ask God to make you loving and giving. Ask Him for help to give what you can and not to ignore those who need God's help.

❖ Ask God to make you listen and pay attention to warning words. Ask Him to turn you from the road to hell to His way of life and hope in Christ.

9.　★ Thank God that He is a living powerful God and that no one is more powerful than He.

❖ Ask God to show you that He had to send His Son to die on the cross for sinners like you.

10.   ★ Thank God that there is nothing that can overthrow Him and that whatever happens, those who trust in Him need not fear as their souls are safe with Him.
❖ Ask God to bring you to a belief in Him and His power and a knowledge of your need for Him in all things.

11.   ★ Thank the Lord that He will never disappoint or fail us. He will never reject us if we come humbly to Him in Christ. Ask the Lord that you would love Him because He loved you first. Thank Him for this most wonderful gift of salvation.
❖ Trust in the Lord. Ask Him to show you that the way you think is not the way He thinks and that by nature we disobey God and go the wrong way. Ask Him to do what is necessary to bring you back to His way.

12.   ★ Ask God to make you a strong witness so that those who mock God and resent Him will see in your life the great peace they are missing.
❖ Ask God to convict you when you see the lives of others who love Him. Ask Him to make you want the peace and joy they have. Ask Christ to convict your soul and make it submissive to Him.

13.   ★ Thank God that He lives for ever; He is eternal and never-ending. Thank Him that though your life passes, and your friends and family die, He and His Word will never end.
❖ Ask God to give you eternal life and salvation. Approach God humbly and plead with Him to save your soul so that when you die, your life will be spent in heaven with Him.

14. ★ Ask God to make you a ready listener to His Word and His voice.
❖ Ask God to convict you of the reality that God speaks to His people and that He has instructions for you personally. If you have not obeyed His command to believe in the Lord Jesus Christ, God's Son, ask God to give you His grace to do this.

15. ★ Ask God to forgive you for your impatience. Ask Him to help you understand that His timing is perfect and that He knows what each of His children need.
❖ Ask the Lord to save you from living a life without Him and spending eternity without Him. Ask Him to make you willing to talk about Christ and listen to His teachings.

16. ★ Ask God to teach you to pray. Thank Him for the gifts He has given you that you did not ask for. Thank Him that He knows you better than you know yourself and knows exactly what you need. Thank Him that you can speak to Him at any time about anything.
❖ Ask the Lord to forgive your sins for Jesus' sake. Thank God that Christ's sacrifice made this wonderful salvation possible.

17. ★ Take every anxiety to God. Tell Him how thankful you are for His love and holiness.
❖ Ask the Lord to protect your heart and mind from sinful and wicked thoughts and longings.

18. ★ Thank God that He forgives sinners and is willing to use saved sinners to bring others to the knowledge of Christ. Ask God to use you to tell people about Him and His Son.

❖ Thank God for godly parents. Ask God to help you honor your parents by listening to and acting on what they teach you about God. Seek grace to honor the Lord by submitting to Him, so that you want to give your life to Him and live your life for Him. If your parents do not love God pray for their salvation, too. Pray that your whole family will come to know God savingly.

19. ★ Thank God for loving you even when you were His enemy and had no regard for Him. Thank Him for changing you to love Him instead of hating Him.
❖ Ask the Lord to change you to someone who loves God from your heart and not just someone who says the right things but doesn't mean them.

20. ★ Thank the Lord for His mercy when He saves you from your sin and remembers it no more. Ask Him to make you remember His instructions and corrections. Ask Him for His help to conquer sin in your life.
❖ Ask the Lord to convict you of the sin of taking His name in vain. Ask Him to forgive you and keep your soul for eternity.

21 ★ Thank God that His compassion for us was so great that He sent His Son, Jesus Christ, to this earth as a baby, to later suffer and die on the cross. Thank Him that He loved His people so much that even when they were wicked sinners He felt sorry for them and determined to give them salvation.
❖ Ask the Lord to prick your conscience and alert you to the sins in your life. Ask the Lord to take charge of your life.

22.   ★ Ask God to give you a positive attitude toward helping others. Ask Him to make you willing to give even when it inconveniences you and means real sacrifice.
❖ Ask God to keep control of your temper. Ask for forgiveness for selfishness and anger. Ask Him to change you from within and bring you to Himself.

23.   ★ Pray to God to make your desires godly. Ask Him to give you a desire to spend time with Him and with His people and His Word.
❖ Ask God to free you from the captivity of sin and make you His child. Pray to Him that He will not only convict you of your sin but show you the truth of His love and His holiness.

24.   ★ Ask God to persuade you of His love. Thank Him for sending His Son to die on the cross for salvation. Ask Him to bring you to a certain faith and knowledge of this personally.
❖ Pray to God for forgiveness for those times that you have doubted Him, His power, and perhaps even His existence. Pray that in reading His Word and in prayer He will show you Himself and convict you of the sin of doubting.

25.   ★ Thank God for His power that He can change a wicked sinner into a godly follower of Christ. Pray that He will do that in your life.
❖ Pray to God that He will show you the dark, stained, sinful life that you lead and bring you to your knees in repentance and desire for salvation.

26. ★Pray to God that you will give a strong testimony to others of what God has done in your life. Ask Him to make you bold for Jesus Christ and that when death comes you will be strong and at peace with Christ.

❖ Ask God to convict you of your sin and make you ready for eternity by trusting in His Son Jesus Christ. Then ask God to make it clear to you that you are a Christian and belong to Him.

27. ★Ask God to be merciful to you and to forgive your sins today. Ask Him to help you learn from mistakes as well as His Word and to please Him more in the future.

❖ Ask God to show you your sins and your need to humbly approach Him for forgiveness. Ask Him to show you that there is nothing in you that is worthy of salvation and that all good gifts come from God.

Scripture Index for Book 5

17. 1 Samuel 5:1-6:16
     Philippians 4:6-7

18. Ecclesiastes 11

19. Romans 12: 3-21

20. Acts 4:13-22
     James 3:10

21. 1 Timothy 1:12-17

22. Genesis 4:1-15

23. Genesis 6:5
     Song of Solomon 1:5
     Isaiah 53:4-5
     Romans 8:31-39

24. 2 Kings 4:1-7

25. Hebrews 9:16-21

26. Numbers 6:22-26
     1 Samuel 3:1-10
     Job 19:25-27
     Psalms 23 & 24; Psalm 116:1 & 2
     Proverbs 4:14 & 24

27. Luke 18:9-14

Answers to questions

1. He knew that it was his duty to do so.

2. She cast her burden on the Lord in prayer; Balaam's ass; wild goats; wild ass; unicorn; peacocks; ostrich; horse; hawk; eagle; leviathan.

3. Discuss.

4. Visiting the sick and speaking to them of eternity.

5. Discuss.

6. For personal application.

7. We can worship and pray to Him and read His Word.

8. The warning words which turned him to Christ.

9. She placed all her trust and confidence in Him.

10. Elijah.

11. For personal application.

12. God was responsible for sending Bruce with the bread through his providence. Joy.

13. Discuss.

14. Elijah.

15. He remembered the prayer taught him as a child.

16. Discuss. You can pray anywhere at any time.

17. His trust in God for everything.

18. It was brought on by conviction of sin and cured by forgiveness from Jesus.

19. No, he gained a friend and learned to follow Jesus Christ.

20. Swearing is against God's law and sinful.

21. They both trusted in Jesus and wanted him to trust, too. The girl's words were used by God to awaken the prisoner's conscience and bring back the teaching he had received in his youth.

22. Very different. He had learned to control his temper and to take responsibility for his actions.

23. Jesus is so good and kind and has promised not to cast out any who come to Him (John 6:37).

24. Elijah and the widow (1 Kings 17:9-24).

25. The Bible says so in Psalm 51:7 and Revelation 7:14.

26. Jesus. They know that Jesus Christ is their Redeemer and has saved them from their sins and that He is alive. They know that they will see Him and that their bodies will be resurrected from the grave.

27. For personal application.

Scripture Index for Books 1-5

Book number given in bold, page number after it in normal text

OLD TESTAMENT

Joshua	7	**3**	147
	24:14-28	**4**	71
Judges	14:1-16	**3**	159
Ruth	1:15-18:1	**4**	84
1 Samuel	2:30	**3**	27
	3:1-10	**5**	137
	5:1- 6:16	**5**	78
	17:1-58	**4**	132
	20	**3**	28
	23:13-29	**5**	48
2 Samuel	9	**2**	61
1 Kings	8:22-30	**3**	19
	17	**3**	65
	17:1-7	**1**	60
	17:1-16	**5**	29
	18:20-40	**2**	38
	22	**3**	70
2 Kings	4:1-7	**5**	126
	5:1-14	**4**	48
	5:42-44	**5**	17
	7:13-23	**3**	95
1 Chronicles	29:14	**3**	22
2 Chronicles	7:14	**3**	53
	24	**3**	77
	30:9	**1**	63
	33:1-20	**2**	146
Ezra	7:10	**1**	75
Nehemiah	8:10	**5**	56
Esther	2	**5**	74
	8	**5**	56
Job	19:25-27	**2**	137
	39	**5**	17
	41:1-11	**5**	17
Psalms	9:7-14	**1**	95

Psalms			
12	**1**	105
19	**1**	85
19:7-11	**1**	104
19:30	**4**	147
23	**5**	133
24	**5**	133
27:10	**1**	125
34	**2**	64
34:11-22	**2**	124
34:15-22	**3**	159
34:17	**2**	64
37:5	**1**	40
40	**2**	153
50:15	**3**	163
50:17	**4**	38
51	**2**	117
51:11	**3**	41
66:18	**1**	36
66:20	**4**	67
68:1-10	**4**	79
68:5	**5**	15
79	**1**	43
79:8-9	**3**	91
80:3	**3**	91
89:1-10	**3**	114
91	**5**	22
91:3	**2**	68
91:4	**2**	64
103:10-12	**4**	121
107:17-32	**2**	111
107:20	**1**	130
107:30	**2**	102
108:4	**4**	40
115	**5**	31

Psalms	116:1-2	5	137
	119:46-56	1	109
	119:65-72	3	118
	119:97-104	1	122
	119:97-105	1	52
	119:105-112	1	75
	121	2	143
	124	3	120
	131	1	56
	133:1	3	61
	139:7-12	4	84
	142:7	3	59
	146:4	1	78
	146:5	5	17
	147:2	3	59
Proverbs	1:8-19	1	25
	1:33	3	120
	3:1-12	5	50
	4:14	5	125
	4:24	5	126
	11:1-6	3	34
	11:13	1	66
	13:15	3	18
	15:16	1	57
	17:7	4	35
	18:24	4	35
	19:17	1	85
	23:32	2	78 & 79
	29:25	5	22
Ecclesiastes	9:10	4	53
	11	5	84
	11:1	1	85
		2	74 & 79
		5	84

Jonah	1&2	**4**	84
Micah	7:18-19	**4**	121
	7:18	**4**	40
Nahum	1:7	**2**	117
Habakkuk	2:18-20	**2**	38
	3:2	**2**	124
Zephaniah	2:12-13	**3**	70
	3:17	**1**	85
Haggai	1:12-13	**2**	111
Zechariah	3	**2**	79
	3:2	**2**	79
Malachi	3:16-18	**4**	67

NEW TESTAMENT

Matthew	1:21	**4**	65
	4:6	**3**	91
	4:18-22	**2**	89
	5	**3**	103
	5:7	**3**	107
	5:34	**3**	48
	5:38-48	**2**	22
	6:5-15	**1**	41
		3	61
	6:19-20	**3**	70
	6:19-21	**4**	90
	6:26-34	**5**	25
	6:33	**2**	101
	7:12	**2**	51
		3	114
	7:13-14	**4**	117
	9:5	**4**	60
	10:19	**4**	40
	10:27-31	**5**	20
	10:29	**2**	141

Romans	8:31-39	**5**	121
	9:25-26	**3**	156
	11:33	**4**	112
	12:1-21	**3**	22
	12:3-21	**5**	91
	12:14	**1**	27
	12:20	**5**	85
1 Corinthians	2:6-16	**2**	50
	4:11-16	**1**	27
	6:19-20	**1**	119
	8:4-6	**2**	38
	9:16-23	**2**	18
	10:13	**1**	63
	12:19-24	**1**	66
	15:33	**4**	23
	15:56-57	**2**	95
2 Corinthians	2:13	**4**	40
	5:17	**2**	101
	6:2	**4**	93
	6:17-18	**4**	43
	12:19-24	**1**	66
Galatians	3:21-29	**1**	99
	5:19-26	**2**	148
Ephesians	2:8	**1**	78
	5:26	**1**	105
	6:5-9	**4**	76
	6:13	**4**	101
Philippians	2:14	**1**	57
	4:4-9	**1**	40
	4:6-7	**5**	78
	4:6	**5**	25
	4:8	**3**	128
Colossians	2:8	**1**	25
	3:2	**4**	90

Acknowledgements

All of the Christian stories contained in these books are based on true happenings, most of which occurred in the nineteenth century. We have gleaned them from a variety of sources, including several books by Richard Newton, then rewrote them in contemporary language. Many of them are printed here for the first time; others were previously printed, without the accompanying devotional material, in a series titled *Building on the Rock* by the Netherlands Reformed Book and Publishing and by Reformation Heritage Books in the 1980s and 1990s.

Thanksgiving is rendered to God first of all for His help in preparing this series of books. Without Him we can do nothing. We would also like to thank James W. Beeke for supplying some helpful material; Jenny Luteyn, for contributing several of the stories; Jeff Anderson for his illustrations; and Catherine Mackenzie, for her able and invaluable editing. Finally, we would like to thank our loyal spouses, Mary Beeke and Chris Kleyn, for their love, support, and encouragement as we worked on these books over several years. We pray earnestly that the Lord will bless these stories to many hearts.

Joel R. Beeke and Diana Kleyn
Grand Rapids, Michigan

Author Information

Dr. Joel R. Beeke is president and professor of systematic theology and homiletics at Puritan Reformed Theological Seminary, pastor of the Heritage Netherlands Reformed Congregation in Grand Rapids, Michigan, editor of Banner of Sovereign Grace Truth, editorial director of Reformation Heritage Books, president of Inheritance Publishers, and vice-president of the Dutch Reformed Translation Society. He has written or edited fifty books (including several for children), and contributed fifteen hundred articles to Reformed books, journals, periodicals, and encyclopedias. His Ph.D. is in Reformation and Post-Reformation theology from Westminster Theological Seminary. He is frequently called upon to lecture at seminaries and to speak at Reformed conferences around the world. He and his wife Mary have been blessed with three children.

Diana Kleyn is a member of the Heritage Netherlands Reformed Congregation in Grand Rapids, Michigan. She is married to Chris, is the mother of three children, and has a heart for helping children understand and embrace the truths of God's Word. She is the author of *Taking Root and Bearing Fruit*, stories about conversions and godliness written for children. She and Dr. Beeke have recently co-authored Reformation Heroes, which tells the life story of about forty Reformation figures for children ten years and older. She also writes monthly for the children's section in *The Banner of Sovereign Grace Truth*.

Building on the Rock
Books 1-5

Book 1
How God Used a Thunderstorm
Living for God and The Value of Scripture

Book 2
How God Stopped the Pirates
Missionary Tales and Remarkable Conversions

Book 3
How God Used a Snowdrift
Honoring God and Dramatic Deliverances

Book 4
How God Used a Drought and
an Umbrella
Faithful Witnesses and Childhood Faith

Book 5
How God Sent a Dog to Save a Family
God's Care and Childhood Faith

Other books published by Christian
Focus Publications in connection with
Reformation Heritage Books.

*Bible Questions and Answers
for Children* by Carine Mackenzie
ISBN 978-1-85792-702-3
and
Teachers' Manual by Diana Kleyn
ISBN 978-1-85792-701-6

Bible Stories and Non Fiction

Bible Time, Bible Wise, Bible Alive and
The Bible Explorer
All by Carine Mackenzie

Paul - Journeys of Adventure
ISBN: 978-1-85792-465-7

Noah - Rescue Plan
ISBN: 978-1-85792-466-4

Joseph - God's Dreamer
ISBN: 978-1-85792-343-8

Esther - The Brave Queen
ISBN: 978-1-84550-195-2

Mary - The Mother of Jesus
ISBN: 978-1-84550-168-6

Gideon - Soldier of God
ISBN: 978-1-84550-196-9

The Bible Explorer: 978-1-85792-533-3

BIBLE ALIVE SERIES

Jesus the Storyteller
ISBN: 978-1-85792-750-4

Jesus the Child
ISBN: 978-1-85792-749-4

Jesus the Saviour
ISBN: 978-1-85792-754-2

Jesus the Healer
ISBN: 978-1-85792-751-1

Jesus the Miracle Worker
ISBN: 978-1-85792-752-8

Jesus the Teacher
ISBN: 978-1-85792-753-5

**Fiction books with God's message
of truth
Freestyle – 12+
Flamingo – 9-12
Fulmar – 7-10 years
Check out our webpage for further
details: www.christianfocus.com**

Martin's Last Chance
ISBN: 978-1-85792-425-1

A Different Mary
ISBN: 978-0-90673-195-6

Sarah & Paul Make a Scrapbook
ISBN: 978-1-87167-635-8

The Broken Bow
ISBN: 978-1-87167-698-3

The Big Green Tree at No. 11
ISBN: 978-1-85792-731-3

TRAILBLAZERS

The Complete Classic Range:
Worth Collecting

Saved at Sea
ISBN: 978-1-85792-795-5

A Basket of Flowers
ISBN: 978-1-85792-525-8

Christie's Old Organ
ISBN: 978-1-85792-523-4

A Peep Behind the Scenes
ISBN: 978-1-85792-524-1

Little Faith
ISBN: 978-1-85792-567-8

Children's Stories
by D L Moody
ISBN: 978-1-85792-640-8

Mary Jones and Her Bible
ISBN: 978-1-85792-568-5

Children's Stories by J C Ryle
ISBN: 978-1-85792-639-2

Childhood's Years
ISBN: 978-1-85792-713-9

The Adventures Series
An ideal series to collect

Have you ever wanted to visit the rainforest? Have you ever longed to sail down the Amazon river? Would you just love to go on Safari in Africa? Well these books can help you imagine that you are actually there.

Pioneer missionaries retell their amazing adventures and encounters with animals and nature. In the Amazon you will discover Tree Frogs, Piranha Fish and electric eels. In the Rainforest you will be amazed at the Armadillo and the Toucan. In the blistering heat of the African Savannah you will come across Lions and elephants and hyenas. And you will discover how God is at work in these amazing environments.

CHRISTIAN FOCUS PUBLICATIONS

Christian Focus | Christian Heritage | CF4K | Mentor

Christian Focus Publications publishes books for adults and children under its four main imprints: Christian Focus, Christian Heritage, CF4K and Mentor. Our books reflect that God's word is reliable and Jesus is the way to know him, and live for ever with him.

Our children's publication list includes a Sunday School curriculum that covers pre-school to early teens; puzzle and activity books. We also publish personal and family devotional titles, biographies and inspirational stories that children will love.

If you are looking for quality Bible teaching for children then we have an excellent range of Bible story and age specific theological books.

From pre-school to teenage fictions, we have it covered.

Find us at our web page:
www.christianfocus.com

Reformation Heritage Books

2919 Leonard St, NE, Grand Rapids, MI, 49525
Phone: 616-977-0599; Fax: 616-285-3246
email: orders@heritagebooks.org
Website: www.heritagebooks.org